ROAD
TO NOWHERE

ROAD
TO NOWHERE

JIM FUSILLI

THOMAS & MERCER

Text copyright © 2012 Jim Fusilli

Published by Thomas & Mercer
P.O. Box 400818
Las Vegas, NV 89140

ISBN-13: 9781612185972
ISBN-10: 1612185975

To Peter Spiegelman

PROLOGUE

Manfredi said, "She'll adjust," but no, that never sounded right. It seemed a playbook answer, generic. With Pup, nothing off the shelf ever worked. He was certain it wasn't going to start working now.

He didn't blame the marshals. They'd done everything they could. The North Cascades were a wonder: the vistas, the bracing air, dappled sunlight, pine needles underfoot. He bought an old Jeep and drove with his daughter deep into the Wenatchee forest. Two alone, they stood in silence on a bluff as if to absorb the boundless beauty. But they were thinking the same thing: we don't belong. Of all the places in the country Manfredi and the U.S. marshals could've chosen, they'd recommended an evergreen Eden that could not fail to remind them of what they'd lost. They'd lost everything. Especially him. Because soon Pup would be gone too.

They climbed toward the clouds to view Lake Chelan from a distance, and when they came to a barren stretch a sudden gust jostled them. He lost his footing, the side of his sneaker catching on a length of shale. But he recovered quickly. Pup's hair — long, lighter than her mother's, darker than his — flapped and flew until she pulled it back, tied it with a rubber band. Despite her down jacket she shivered, and he put his arm on her shoulder and without a word she reached up, lifted his wrist and slipped his embrace. She said let's go and he nodded and they turned their backs to beauty. She walked ahead. He called her name…

She was 16, so he tossed her the keys to the Jeep.

She caught them and held them at arm's length so he could retrieve them.

Out here, he told her, you'll have to drive.

She nodded. Later, she said, "Grandpa showed me how to drive."

"I didn't know."

She shrugged. She said, "I told Mom."

She kept her own counsel since the day she was born. A quiet, thoughtful infant with a furrowed brow. She studied her toys. She observed the characters on television. She did the requisite things children do, at least according to her mother. He had never had siblings; all children were a mystery to him, Pup only more so. She seemed solemn at times, always earnest; rarely was there a light moment. It seemed every action had added importance for her. He asked, "What is it, Pup?" She shook her head just so.

"Is she unhappy?" he asked her mother.

"Are you unhappy?" Moira replied. They were in bed. He faced her, his head propped in his palm, his elbow digging into the mattress. He had a teardrop scar at the corner of his right eye.

"No. Why?"

"She's just like you."

"That's not—"

"She is. It's uncanny. Don't you see it?"

He decided to drive down to the Smithsonian, a father-daughter trip while Moira prepared for the first days of school. A cloudy morning; rain threatened but never quite arrived. Pup was in a child's seat in back. She stared out the window, her hands folded on her lap. At one point, she slipped off her sneakers and socks. She put the sneakers side by side next to her, a sock in each.

They crossed into Delaware. He looked into the rearview mirror. He said, "Pup—"

She held up her finger. Forty minutes later, as they passed an exit for Havre de Grace, Maryland, she said, "What did you say?"

Her classmates played in Central Park and Pup sat on a bench with a marble notebook, pencil between her teeth.

Teachers loved her. She did her work, never quarreled, helped when asked. They attributed her amenable nature to her mother's position as a teacher in a school in the Bronx. She respects the profession, said one when Pup was in the second grade.

"Thank you, but no," Pup replied to the clown who offered her a balloon at a block party off Riverside Drive.

He saw that her friends invited her along when they gathered, but knew she wouldn't participate. They made excuses for her. She likes to read — that was one. Her father was another.

"She's impenetrable, I guess," he said in reply to one of the mothers outside her school.

"Is that good?"

Works for me, he thought, not realizing he'd left the woman hanging in silence.

When she was eight years old, Pup set out to make a Halloween costume. Moira volunteered to help; with Pup, it was like that: you had to ask if she would allow you to assist. Otherwise she'd think you didn't believe she could do it herself.

Pup in her room with patterns she'd downloaded. A sewing kit, safety scissors, two-sided tape. Such ambition, her mother said.

"She wants to be you for Halloween," Moira told him.

She took Pup to a restaurant-supply shop on the Bowery, to a store that sold costumes in the East Village. Pup, he was told, sampled, compared. She negotiated.

She dressed in a chef's coat, white pants and white Crocs, a spatula in her fist. A little toque with her name written in magic marker on the paper above her brow.

Pup misunderstood his work. She thought he was in charge. Maybe he'd let her think that when she visited the restaurant. He was a line cook. He worked the grill. He'd had a thousand jobs in his life. This was one of them. He was in charge of nothing.

On Pup's 11th birthday, she began writing a novel.

"What's it about?" her mother asked a few weeks later.

Pup said she didn't know. It wasn't done yet. There's a man. He's misunderstood. Maybe he's magical. He has a scar. I don't know...

Later, Moira came to bed dressed in summer attire — a T-shirt, nothing more. "Did you hear her? Seven sentences," she said as she pulled back the top sheet. "A chatterbox, this one."

A few minutes later, he said, "Huh?"

It was 3 o'clock in the morning and he was dragging red and raw after a difficult shift, but there she was in the alley behind the restaurant. Moira smiled; she said, "We're driving to the Cape."

Fourteen years, she said. It's a big deal.

The car she rented was at the curb out front.

They'd hit a rough patch. She'd done nothing wrong.

"You can't say no," she added, a bottle of Veuve Clicquot in her hand.

Pup?

At Moira's parents'. Her father, a lawyer, hired an agent. Pup's manuscript sold.

He sighed. He trudged toward her. He said, "The Cape it is…" He leaned in to kiss her cheek. "Happy anniversary."

She screamed. He turned, heard the shot, saw blood spray out the side of the man's head. The Champagne bottle crashed to the cobblestone.

He told her. He said, "You don't have to testify."

"But you didn't see it. I did."

"The man is dangerous."

"We've been over this."

"It's dangerous."

"Again with the dangerous." She stood. She paced the kitchen. Pup was listening. They knew she was.

He laid it out for Moira again. "Like I said, I'll be you, you be me. I saw. Your back was to it."

"You'll lie to the grand jury. Under oath."

"To protect you? Yes."

"That's wrong."

As simple as that. Black and white.

He said it again. "I was facing him. You were facing me."

She said no.

She said, "My father says it's never going to go to trial."

"Your father is a corporate attorney."

"The testimony is sealed."

"Moira, the hitter saw us."

"The hitter?"

"These guys. They don't forget."

She said, "So now you're an expert."

She stood too. He went to her. They'd done this before. The exact same deal. Yes, no. Pup is the stubborn one in this little family?

"We both testify," she said. "Our testimony puts him away. *Our* testimony."

He took her in his arms.

She whispered, "I don't want you standing alone."

I could not begin to tell you how many times I've been by myself, he thought. The past 14 years have been a miraculous exception. More than I expected. More than I deserve.

She said, "Let's go together and put an end to this."

Pup said, "I'm going with you."

He said, "You stay with Grandma."

Pup held her grandfather's hand as they entered the courthouse.

She waited as her mother was called.

Moira returned. It's done, she said.

Later, Pup said her mother was shaking when she sat next to her.

He kissed her on the head when he returned from his testimony. He heard the shot. He turned. He saw the man with the gun. That man. The defendant. Yes, he was certain. Of course.

If they had asked, he could've told them the gun's make and model.

They left together; now he was holding his daughter's hand. As they were about to enter the limousine, he saw a man standing at the curb, his topcoat fluttering in the November wind.

The man glared at them.

Clearly, he was the defendant's son. Built the same; same features. Taller, his hair not yet bearing a touch of gray.

He exuded menace. He invited the thought that he was a thug like his old man, who, it turned out, had been paid to kill the man in the alley.

Through the pedestrian traffic, over cars and taxis, he kept watching. Pup slipped in, Moira slipped in.

His father-in-law called to him.

"Wait," he replied. "I'll be a minute."

He looked at the thug without hostility. He posed no threat. He merely wanted to see if he could determine what the man was thinking or feeling. He saw nothing.

Later he would claim the man looked at him with cold rage. But it was nothing. A machine.

Well trained, said Manfredi, as they packed up the apartment. Programmed. Since childhood.

Before he and Pup moved west, Pup had an offer from a producer in Hollywood. Her book about the enigmatic Nathaniel Hill hadn't sold well, but that said more about the state of old publishing than it did about the book. If Pup hadn't insisted that no one know she was a teenager and had begun writing Nathaniel Hill's tale when she was 11, the sales story might've been different.

But, said Michael Koons, her Hollywood agent, water under the bridge…

Pup had published the book under an alias.

"It stands on its own," she'd said.

Now she had another alias, one supplied by the U.S. marshals.

"I need you here," Koons told her.

Manfredi said, "If she wants a public life, we're going to have to back-engineer a profile."

"Dad, it's no good," she said.

He trusted no one now. The waitresses were listening. The family in the booth behind them. The girl with the menus who sat them by the window: she was calling New York now. They're here, she was saying. In plain sight.

The man who killed Moira, the thug's son, was in custody. Held over for trial, Manfredi said. But the men who hired the old man, they're out there. Speaking like it was me, Manfredi added, I don't know, maybe you're better off someplace new?

Safety wasn't the only issue.

"Whose lives are these?" Pup asked.

"I know," he said. He could feel himself falling apart. If not for Pup, he would allow himself to drift away.

From the cabin's back porch, Pup stared toward the trees. She didn't know when he was watching or when he was gone.

Later, he prodded the fire. Sparks fell as the flames rose. Shadows danced.

He took a walk in the forest. He sat on a stump, he stared at his hands. Nightfall arrived. He made his way back to the cabin with only his cell phone shining a light on a path, the stars far above the pines.

"Pup?" he said when he came in. "Pup?"

She didn't know he'd been gone.

A few days later, or weeks later, he woke up and the Jeep was missing. Some of her clothes too. Her laptop. Her files, her notebooks. Pup had moved on. Nothing of value remained.

She sent him a text. "It's at Sea-Tac." Telling him she'd flown away.

He didn't call Manfredi.

"Is Pup there?" he asked his father.

"Didn't I tell you never to call here?" his old man replied.

He called New York.

"Why didn't you stop her?" his mother-in-law asked.

Pup or Moira?

He tried to hold on, but he was fading fast. Everything he'd gained since he met Moira was slipping away. He was becoming the man he was before they met.

"Gray's Anatomy" at a used bookstore in Wenatchee.

With intensity and care, he tapped into his femoral artery, hissing in pain.

Blood soaked into the floorboards.

He drove north and when the Jeep was as high in the Entiat Mountains as he could go, he removed the bandages and let blood dribble onto the driver's seat. He smeared a bit onto the steering wheel.

He let the Jeep roll off a ledge and bounce down into a ravine.

Then he disappeared.

CHAPTER 1

He was minding his own business. Nobody was bothering him. The L was crowded — an unexpected cloudburst hurried pedestrians off the Chicago streets — but he'd been boxing the Loop since 4 o'clock. He'd seen rush hour come and go. Night had arrived. The train rattled. It was steamy inside and it squealed when it left Clark on its way to Washington, but not enough to shake him. Strangers coming and going at each stop meant nothing to him and he meant nothing to them. No one knew how long he'd been there. No one asked him what he was thinking or why he didn't speak or smile. No one looked twice. If they had they would've seen a tall, wiry man with sandy hair and a blank expression, alternately gazing at the passing buildings or someone inside the car. For the last few minutes, he'd been watching a nurse's aide struggle to keep awake, the train's sway lolling her to sleep. He'd bet she'd earned her rest, a double shift maybe, 14 hours on her feet carrying the weight of someone else's woes. A hospital couldn't operate without them. They kept the place running. They were miracle workers, and humble.

The rain stopped. A waterfall rushed along the window when the train turned, sluicing from the rooftop, ending in teardrops. He could hear the wheels grind. Chains rattled.

Then, beyond the edge of the elevated tracks, maybe three stories above the sidewalk, he saw a young woman in a parking garage. She stood under a light and seemed to be floating against the shadows in the structure. Dressed in a gray business suit, she had opened the car's back door to drop her briefcase inside.

He saw a stocky man in a black, skintight T-shirt come from behind a beam in front of the car next to hers. He stood behind her. A thin, trimmed beard clung to his jawline.

She closed the car door.

As the train moved on, the man in the garage grabbed the young woman by the shoulder, spun her, reared and punched her in the face. The woman fell backward like a toppled tree, her head striking the concrete floor.

Then the train turned again. A yellow-brick building blocked the view.

The man on the L stood and stepped into the aisle, his fingers pressed against the ceiling for balance.

He got out at the next station, wading hurriedly through a group of teenage girls. Wet newspaper pages were strewn along the platform. At the bottom of the wooden stairs, he stepped around a sagging homeless man, piss-scented and broken.

If the world worked like it should, a CPD patrol car would be parked on the other side of the street, two cops in short sleeves. He'd tell them what he'd seen: a young woman assaulted in the parking garage, third floor. She's hurt. The man: squat, bearded, black hair, dark eyes, dressed in black. Latin. Mexican, maybe. I don't know.

The cop in the passenger seat would look up. "You sure?" Then he'd look over at his partner. They'd be annoyed; they didn't need this, a shit night, the rain cleans nothing. But then their thoughts would run and they'd figure they'd better check it out, given this guy here was sober, clean and forthright, probably educated too. Meaning he knew how to bitch up a ladder, post a grievance online that Internal Affairs or the press would read.

"Stick around," the cop in the passenger seat would say. "Mister..."

The man would give a false name and, when the patrol car pulled out, walk away. Very likely he would never think again about the young woman who took the punch. Maybe he'd see her punished in his dreams. He couldn't control them, no more now than before.

But the man knew the world didn't work like it should. If it did, the woman wouldn't have been assaulted. He wouldn't be hurrying toward the garage, clinging to buildings, backlit by barroom neon. He wouldn't be alone in Chicago.

Water dripped here, streamed there, rolled down the L's rusted stanchions. The scent of sparks followed him, the scent of cats. Steam rose from the streets. Cars drove by, water splashed and then resettled, and he found the parking garage.

He walked past the cashier, her face melting in boredom as she doled out change to a tired man in a dress shirt, his tie at half-mast, jacket hooked on a finger and up by his shoulder.

The man who left the train kept walking, using the incline rather than the stairs. On the second level, a car pulled up behind him and then turned into a parking spot, wet tires squealing.

There were many empty spaces. Commuters had gone for the night.

There she was, and the blood that flowed out of the back of her head was trickling toward him. She's dead, he thought; he'd seen lifeless bodies before. But as he drew nearer, he heard her breathe. When he stood over her, he saw little bloodstained bubbles on her lips. When they popped, new ones formed.

Her purse lay near the back bumper of the car. He retrieved her cell phone. He scanned the numbers she'd called, then tapped 911.

He gave the operator their location and put the phone on the concrete, the connection still live.

Her money and credit cards were in her wallet. He looked at her driver's license. As he put the wallet down next to the open purse, he saw lying on the pavement an empty keycard envelope with the logo of a national hotel chain, a room number written in green ink. He dipped his fingers into her jacket pocket and removed the keycard.

When he looked down at the young woman, he saw a gruesome knot had already formed on her cheek, and blood was dribbling out of her nose.

He dropped a knee to the damp surface and tugged her skirt until it covered her thighs. One of her shoes had flipped off, and he thought about replacing it, but the heel had broken.

He went to the car — a rental — and saw the key was still in the door lock. He looked in the backseat. It was empty, her briefcase gone. The trunk was empty too.

She moaned.

He looked at her.

That bastard had nailed her good.

There were four hotels in the chain in Chicago. One was nearby, a past-its-prime grand palace that dominated the block. The trip took him back the way he came, and then he turned away from the L. A line of taxis queued along East Monroe.

The bellmen didn't give him a second look. When he entered the vast lobby, its ceiling high above the crowded lounge and long reception desk, he remembered he'd passed through here before. A concierge had recommended Millers Pub for lunch. He spent that afternoon at the Art Institute, lost in "Resting" by Antonio Mancini. Awash in morning light, a young woman with dark cascading hair is nude in bed, her expression adrift between thought and anguish. A guard had to tell him it was time to leave. That was yesterday or two weeks ago.

He had the keycard in his hand. He knew the chain liked to put two in their little envelopes. The guy who took out the young woman had the other. If he didn't discover what he came for in the briefcase, he'd look for it in the room.

The man who had been asked to leave the Art Institute now moved with purpose, his rubber soles squeaking on the hotel lobby's marble flooring. He had learned the hard way that it was best to address such things immediately, to meet violence with violence. To delay was to invite it to strike again.

He took the elevator to the 12th floor and walked the black carpet until the number on the envelope matched the number on a door. He listened, straining over the buzz of the ice machine in a nearby alcove. Then he stepped inside.

He was unarmed, but every hotel room stored at least one weapon. He went to the closet, found it, took it down and sat on the edge of the bed, the thing hanging heavy in his fist. He was thinking he'd have to pull the blow or he'd kill the son of a bitch before he found out whether he needed killing.

He looked around the room, peering through slatted light. It hadn't been touched since the maid did her job hours ago, and yet the young woman — Mary Louise Szarsynski, according to her Wisconsin driver's license — had packed. Her suitcase was next to the chest that held the minibar, its handle high as if she expected to return and roll it out. But she hadn't stored it in the rental car's trunk. She wasn't sure she'd have to leave. She was hoping she wouldn't.

He stood to look into the bathroom to see if she'd put away her toiletries. Then he stopped. He heard a mechanical whir. Someone had put a keycard in the door.

He found a dark niche near the closet.

A second later, the bearded brown-skinned man in the black T-shirt entered. He didn't turn on the light. As the door began to close, he moved to the center of the room. He stood at the edge of the king bed.

He had the briefcase in his hand. He was about to toss it on the bedspread when he heard the door click shut. He turned.

The man who had been on the L swung the iron and caught him flush on the side of the face and head. The guy, unconscious before he hit the bed, bounced and landed on the floor.

The iron's long electrical cord had unraveled. For a moment, he thought maybe he'd use it to bind the man's hands to his feet. But then he realized he'd hit him about as hard as the young woman in the garage had been hit. The man on the floor wasn't going anywhere for a while.

He lifted the man's gun, a Smith & Wesson 910 worth $650 out of the box. Then it took him 15 minutes to rifle the room, and he found, tucked between the mattress and the box spring, a thick manila envelope. He lifted it, slipped it down the back of his black jeans and pulled his gray T-shirt until it was covered. When he bent over to remake the bed, the envelope jutted out like he'd sprouted tail feathers. When he stood tall, it was fine.

He dragged the unconscious man by the heels to the alcove with a groaning ice machine. He retrieved Mary Louise Szarsynski's suitcase and rolled it to the elevator, confident the room she'd rented looked as it did when the maid tidied it, save for the blood that had sunk into the dark carpet. He had his fist curled around her briefcase handle. He'd already looked inside and taken out a business card that belonged to somebody else.

When the elevator door opened, there was a couple near the back wall, teenagers dressed fine in Western gear. Holding his girl's hand, the young man wore a stern expression. He was trying to be on top of things, detached and in charge, pimples on his chin. When he tipped the brim of his cowboy hat, he said, "Evening, sir."

The man nodded his reply. The girl smiled, shy and proud.

He unzipped a pouch in the suitcase and stuffed the manila envelope inside.

When the elevator settled in the lobby, he let the young couple pass and slid the pistol snug and low down the back of his jeans. On East Monroe, he flipped both keycards into a trash can and then rolled the suitcase over to the parking garage, the briefcase swaying at his side. The L roared and rattled overhead. Summer rain had become a fine mist.

At the garage, the attendant told him she couldn't remember which EMS company rolled up with CPD.

CHAPTER 2

They took her to Northwestern Memorial. The metal detectors at every entrance meant he had to bury the pistol in a planter in a vest-pocket park off Erie. The soil was muddy and it lodged under his fingernails. He told security at the ER he was a cabbie who was dropping off clothes for a patient. Down the hall, he washed, studied his face in the mirror, ran his clean fingers through his hair and set out to the nurses' station.

He told the nurse he was Mary Louise Szarsynski's brother-in-law. He had to drop off her clothes. She'd want them when she came to.

No place to put them, he was told. She hadn't been assigned a room yet.

Meaning she was spending the night.

He asked and was told a concussion, an ankle sprain. Facial contusions.

But no, he couldn't leave the luggage or the suitcase. Policy. Sorry.

One of the numbers in her cell phone had a 414 area code. He knew the code from a time he'd spent in Milwaukee. The address on her driver's license was West Allis, Wisconsin.

He called it, using the pay phone outside the waiting room.

A woman answered. No, I'm not her mother, she snapped. Sister.

The cops had already notified the family, she told him. Their mother was on their way.

He told Mary Louise Szarsynski's sister he had her clothes. The hospital wouldn't let him leave them. He didn't mention the envelope.

Wait for my mother, she said, annoyed. You can do that. Jesus.

He bought a novel in the hospital's bookstore and devoured it while he had a turkey on fresh ciabatta bread up on the second floor. He could've gone for a beer, but what the hell. For a while, he forgot who he was.

Visitors' hours were over. He nodded to the luggage and was told Mary Louise Szarsynski's mother had arrived. He said he'd be five minutes and he meant it. In and out and gone. The nurse pointed and he rolled the bag along the linoleum.

The woman in the bed nearest the door was old, her parchment skin tugged tight over her tiny frame. She fixed her rheumy eyes on him. Hope flickered. She began to smile. But then, no. He wasn't who she'd hoped for. He was somebody else, neither family, friend nor messenger of death.

The young woman was in the bed behind the dividing curtain, and her mother was holding her hand. The side of the young woman's face was a sickly yellow. It had purpled by her eye. She appeared to be asleep, and he couldn't see if the back of her head was bandaged. Her right ankle was, and propped on a pillow.

Her mother was short, portly, a bright-pink sweater bulging here and there, sensible sandals. Same chestnut-brown hair as her daughter, and he wondered if they still called that style a pageboy. She'd put that gift-shop teddy bear holding a heart on the nightstand, nestling it between the phone and the lamp. She'd poured a glass of water, put a straw in it, everything ready for when her daughter awoke.

She turned slowly, as if she hadn't heard him but felt his presence. He saw she'd been crying.

When she moved to stand, he waved for her to stay seated. But she stood anyway.

He told her he was from the hotel. The police had come by. Everything's here, he said. Suitcase, the briefcase. Everything.

She nodded. He nodded too. She seemed confused, almost stunned. There she was, relaxing at home, watching TV and then the phone. Mrs. Szarsynski, this is Sergeant So and So of the Chicago Police Department. Do you have a daughter Mary Louise...

She searched her memory for protocol, and then went for her handbag. A tip. A couple of dollars.

"No thank you," he said. "It's not necessary."

She nodded. Her pocketbook open, she removed a tissue.

He retreated.

"Wait. Please." She followed him into the hall. "Do you know what happened?" she asked, her voice hushed.

He said he'd heard she'd been assaulted in a parking garage. But otherwise, no.

"They didn't take her money or her credit cards," the mother said. "I don't understand."

He wanted to go. He'd done his part. The cops would find the man near the ice machine. Mary Louise Szarsynski could identify him. They'd haggle and agree to a plea of simple assault.

They stood in silence, the hospital sleeping around them.

"My daughter," she said finally, shaking her head. She smiled a little bit, a happy thought returning.

He began to inch away.

"What's your name?" she asked gently.

He said, "Sam."

"Thank everybody, Sam, for Mary Louise and my family. Would you?"

Yes, he said. And then he walked out.

Sam left through the ER. The nine-millimeter pistol was in the planter. He figured he'd retrieve it and keep it until the next time he needed to fly.

As he passed the security checkpoint, he was swept by the whirling lights of an EMS bus. A couple of techs were unloading a gurney. He walked into the steamy night. Summer rain had returned.

When he drew next to the gurney, he looked down. There, strapped in tight, was the guy he smacked with the iron in Mary Louise Szarsynski's hotel room. The guy who punched her, knocked her out, stole her briefcase. He seemed all but dead, his bearded jaw slack, eyelids not quite sealed shut, breathing labored and shallow. Despite the cervical collar, he rattled as the EMS techs rolled him toward the ER.

He waited, thinking he'd find out if he'd killed him.

But then he left. He took the muddy pistol back to the L.

CHAPTER 3

He didn't feel right. It hadn't settled. Something had been left undone.

He took a shower, shaved, changed into a white oxford. He stepped back on the L, and got off at the Roosevelt/State stop. Into another hotel in the chain, this one smaller, without history, cookie-cutter. It didn't matter, not really. He called the hospital, claiming he was a press officer at the hotel chain who needed to know the disposition of the man found unconscious at the property on East Monroe. He insisted, though a nurse said no and her supervisor told him to call media relations in the morning. But finally an intern came on the line, petulant but determined to display what little authority he had. The young doctor accepted flattery, then opened the spout. Fernando Alvarado was in a coma. Fractured skull. Critical but stable. Too early to say.

Next of kin has been notified. A brother. Carlos. He's flying in from Los Angeles. Call media relations in the morning, though, huh?

It was sticky and damp on Roosevelt, and whatever relief the night was supposed to bring hadn't come. He'd walked two blocks and he was sweating. He was thinking he'd cross Grant Park now, go to the lake, find a bench and stare out at the boats on the water, bobbing, waiting. He'd forget about the Willis Tower peering over his shoulder, the grand fortresses on Michigan, and every other massive thing that stood behind him.

It was too late for Carlos Alvarado to fly into O'Hare or Midway until tomorrow morning. But Alvarado was coming and Mary Louise Szarsynski had to know.

He dialed her cell phone number, but there was no answer. He thought about calling the switchboard to reach the phone on her nightstand but he didn't want to wake up the emaciated old woman who was dying by the door, or Mary Louise's mother, who might be curled in a chair, tucked under a rubbery blanket. He didn't need to do that, not yet.

He walked, he sweated. The Magnificent Mile at 1 a.m., 2 a.m., 2:30. The Wrigley Building, the Tribune Tower, the phosphorescent river. The tulips were gone. Stems without bulbs. Delivery trucks, and soon the city was beginning to awaken. Buses on Michigan. Dawn.

Hospitals ran on their own time. Sunrise surgery. A man in a coma, struck by an iron on the side of his head. Skull fracture. Intracranial hematomas. A buzz saw.

He walked to Northwestern Memorial. He knew he looked saggy, his sandy hair a mess. Fatigue showed on his face. He was 40 now, soon to be 41. He didn't give a rat's ass what anybody thought. Hand to God.

What the hell, he'd bury the gun in the same planter, the soil still moist. Upstairs, and he'd tell her. The guy who battered you is in intensive care, and his brother is coming. I don't know. That's all they said.

If she asked, he'd say, he could be coming to grieve. Nothing more than that.

What do you think, Sam?

People. You never know.

Does he blame my daughter for what happened?

If she asked, if her mother asked, he'd say, I don't know the odds. But odds means it can happen.

Judy Szarsynski was outside the ER, arms folded under her ample breasts, pink sweater sleeves to her wrists. She looked left, she looked right, she started walking that way, her daughter's briefcase at her side. Seeing him, she stopped.

"She's gone, Sam."

Gone? He didn't understand.

"When I woke up, the bed was empty and she was gone," she said. "The suitcase too."

She reached and grabbed his forearm.

She didn't know where she went. She didn't know her daughter had been in Chicago.

No, she doesn't live with me. She lives in New York City.

"I fell asleep, Sam."

Carlos Alvarado went to the emergency room, where he was told his brother was in a coma. He could see him, if he wished. Fernando was a riot of tubes and pumps and mechanisms. His head had blown up to the size of a pumpkin. Click-clack, beep-beep, bright green numbers on video screens.

Poor Fernando.

"When will he die?" Carlos asked.

He stepped outside. It was sunny in Chicago, and hot. Oppressive. The trees were thick, their leaves plump and green, the sky pale and cloudless. He dialed a New York number as he paced. The secretary told him Mr. Cherry wasn't available. Carlos Alvarado said he would hold in such a way that the secretary went and pulled Mr. Cherry from his meeting. At lunchtime, she walked up Wall Street, went into the Trinity Church and prayed. Everything was going to hell, and now she'd spoken to the devil.

"I thought you were told never—"

"My brother is in a coma," Carlos Alvarado said. He was dark and stocky like his younger brother, maybe an inch or two shorter. Unruffled, puffed with dignity, he wore Italian loafers and a charcoal-gray suit appropriate for business travel. "They tell me there is a chance he will die."

Cherry dropped into his leather high-back. He held his head, shaved and shining, and massaged his temples. His tie cost $300, his suspenders twice as much. He had a hole in his left sock. "What happened?"

"You tell me, Mr. Cherry."

Mr. Cherry had no idea. "What are we talking about here?" he asked.

"My brother is in a coma," Alvarado repeated. "You said one woman — a girl, you said — and a package. A simple assignment. But now my brother is in a coma."

"*I* said?"

"*Your man* said. Same thing."

"No it's not."

"Yes it is."

Cherry calculated. "The envelope—"

"Maybe the police have it," Alvarado said. He was upset. Sick on the inside; topsy-turvy. As discipline wavered, old feelings were oozing through.

"No they don't," Cherry said. He hadn't gotten a call.

"My brother—"

"Your brother. I understand. Someone attacked him."

Alvarado took a deep breath to center his feelings.

"Before? After?" Cherry asked. "When?"

"That is information Fernando may take to the grave."

"You have to find out."

"No I don't."

"Mr. Alvarado, the task is not yet complete," Cherry said. In his clubby, oak-paneled office, he was impenetrable. There was no problem that couldn't be resolved to his satisfaction. "I was told your work was flawless. And yet, a flaw, Mr. Alvarado."

"I think maybe the police have your package," Alvarado replied. "Maybe they are in the lobby right now, Mr. Francis Cherry. They are in the elevator. Hear it rise. Listen to the footsteps."

"And me, I'm over here thinking now there's an additional stimulus for you. Wouldn't you say? Hello?"

Alvarado had already moved on. Lost in thought, he paced from shade to sun, then began walking with measured steps toward Michigan Avenue. He was thinking objectively about Fernando. There was no one in the organization he could trust as much, as unconditionally. It never occurred to him that he would have to proceed without him. He had no contingency plan. Fernando was going to be with him forever.

Carlos Alvarado, who hadn't been frightened since he was a child, shuddered as he realized he didn't know what to do.

Except kill the son of a bitch who put that savage attack on Fernando. Of course he knew what he had to do with him. Pull his spine out the top of his head. Feed him alive to starving rats.

Sure. No question. Of course. That.

CHAPTER 4

He couldn't talk himself out of it. He wanted to see it through. She'd had a terrible jolt. It bothered him, knowing she'd seen her daughter like that.

He remembered that teddy bear on the night stand, her expression when she stood to give him a tip, the way she told him to say thank you to his colleagues at the hotel.

The police were done with her. Now she was carrying this thing by herself.

He said he'd see her home.

"Oh no, Sam. That's not necessary. Really."

His employer insisted, he said.

He watched as she thought about it.

The hotel. A reputable national chain. They had advertisements on TV, well-lit signs above the highways; for travelers, a beacon in the night. People want to believe. They think they're making a choice.

"The least I can do," he added.

"Are you sure?"

Yes.

She rooted in her pocketbook for the parking receipt. He offered to drive, but she said no. They came up from the underground garage and maneuvered to 90 West to 94, going north toward West Allis, the moon still ghostlike in the bleached morning sky. Rush hour lingered, but they were heading away from it. She said they'd be all right until Waukegan and then they'd find traffic into Kenosha, Racine and Milwaukee.

He'd been on 94 before, drove it up and down. The rest stops were clean, the vending machines well stocked. He liked cities. Milwaukee was fine.

"Do you know what's going on, Sam?"

I did not, no.

"It wasn't random, was it?"

He said he didn't know. But she was right.

"She's afraid. I mean, she wouldn't show it. That girl. Never cautious. Never. Maybe you'd call her fearless. Some people would. But if she's running, she's afraid."

He turned to face her, the seatbelt tugging his shoulder.

She said, "I suppose it's helped her. You know, in school, in her career and so forth, that attitude. She's ambitious."

"What does she do?"

"She works on Wall Street."

Wall Street.

He sat Pup on the bronze bull. They had lunch under the sun on Stone Street. Set on cobblestone, the table wobbled. He drizzled malt vinegar on his French fries, Pup frowning in doubt. Go on, he said, try one.

"An administrative assistant in a financial-services firm. She started as a temp." Judy Szarsynski allowed herself a beam of motherly pride. "That's what I mean: she just goes for it. Didn't know a single soul in New York but…"

She shook her head. "Of course, now she's running. So she's afraid."

She was driving slow and steady, two hands on the wheel, the suspension shot. The old wagon had more than 100,000 miles on the odometer. There was a crocheted throw on the backseat speckled with dog hair.

"And so here we are, Sam. Here we are. She's gotten herself into something."

Right, he thought. She's into something.

"Is that why you brought her suitcase? So she could run?"

He said no.

He said, "But the man who assaulted your daughter is at the hospital. Intensive care."

She took her eyes off the road for a moment to look at him. She'd buried a young husband, raised two daughters, turned down a chance to run off to South Dakota with a man who sold office supplies. She was 52 years old and had seen her share. No one had to tell her twice.

"You did that, Sam? You put him there?"

He didn't reply.

"You helped my daughter. I wouldn't tell."

"She was smart to run. The man has a brother. He's in from Los Angeles."

He wasn't going to mention the envelope and he wasn't going to let her entertain the hope that Fernando Alvarado's brother might be a law-abiding citizen.

"Are they going to keep looking for her? No, you don't have to answer that. She wouldn't have left otherwise."

He'd been thinking about how Alvarado found her in a parking garage. One young woman in a city of nearly three million people.

"I wonder," she said. "I mean, did something happen in New York?"

He was tired. Days were for sleeping. He needed a shower. He didn't want to think about New York anymore.

They fell to thoughtful silence. The engine rattled. The air conditioning did too.

Judy Szarsynski told him she was a secretary at the high school and in the summer worked in a big-box hardware store in New Berlin, on the other side of Route 45.

They left the interstate, got off a highway, found a two-way street, a stop sign, turned. A row of houses, a neighborhood, plain and simple. Telephone wires, newspapers in plastic bags on the steps. Second-hand cars in the driveways, dusty despite the rain.

She pulled into a path next to a bungalow with yellow vinyl siding, white trim and a glassed-in porch. There was another car in front of the garage.

He stretched as he stood. The house sat on a small hill, the slope covered with moist grass. There was an entrance off the driveway. He noticed the light above the door was fixed to a motion detector. So was the light above the garage.

"I live alone," she explained as she gathered her pocketbook and the briefcase. "That's my daughter's car. My other daughter. Bonnie."

Chicago was fine in the summer. Tourists, so he was just another pigeon pecking at seed. In West Allis, he felt eyes staring at him between blinds and shutters.

"How does a cup of fresh coffee sound?" she asked.

It was time to go.

"Sure," he heard himself say. "Sounds good."

A big collie jumped on him. "Henry," she scolded, "get down. Henry!"

"Where is she?" Bonnie demanded. "Where— And who the hell is this?"

"Bonnie…"

"Where is she?"

"Sam, my daughter Bonnie."

Bonnie, angry and wide. Scowling, she looked him up and down.

"He works at the hotel where Mary Louise—"

"Afraid we're going to sue?"

"Bonnie…"

"Where is she?" she repeated. "I thought she was coming with you."

"She has things to do, I guess." Sagging, Judy Szarsynski tossed her keys and handbag on the island. The briefcase went next to the refrigerator. "Sam offered to see me home."

The old rock-band T-shirt didn't flatter Bonnie and neither did the denim cutoffs. The butterfly tattoo on her calf hadn't held up over time. That hairstyle died with the century. The house smelled of cigarettes, but he didn't see an ashtray.

"Why didn't she tell us she was coming to Chicago?"

"She rented a car. Maybe she was going to come by."

She sneered. "She's ashamed of us."

"Bonnie, please… She'll be fine. A mild concussion, bruises, a sprained ankle. She was lucky."

"That's my sister. You bet," Bonnie said, turning to the guest. "Lucky Mary Louise. Life is pretty damned sweet when you only think about yourself."

The dog circled for a spot to settle down, a cool stretch of flooring.

"Sam, let's have that coffee I promised."

Bonnie was still staring at him, suspicious, eager to blame somebody for something. Maybe he'd do. But then a little light went on behind her eyes and she did this thing she thought made her seven different kinds of cute, a change in posture, a smile she hoped raised a dimple.

He saw it. He'd seen it before. Women liked him. It'd been that way since he was 14.

"Where are the kids?" Judy said as she rinsed out the coffee pot.

"Roger's got them."

"My three grandchildren, Sam."

He nodded. Artwork on construction paper and photos in magnet frames.

"Roger runs his own business," Judy said, opening a cabinet. "Heating and ventilation. Air conditioning."

"He pretty much does what he wants," Bonnie said. "Me too."

Judy said, "Sit down, Sam. You must be exhausted."

There was a table with a lazy Susan filled with condiments and paper napkins. But he sat on a stool at the island and dropped his hands on his thighs.

Milwaukee was 15 minutes away by car on 94. Then the Amtrak Hiawatha. He'd be back in Chicago by early afternoon, especially if he avoided the temptation of a couple brats and a beer near the station.

Judy Szarsynski had to go to work. She said she'd drive him to the train, but he knew it was out of her way. "Sam, it's the least I can do." She excused herself and went upstairs to shower.

Bonnie offered him a cigarette. He declined. She waited until she heard the water running before lighting hers.

"So." She wriggled onto the stool next to him. "What's your story? You that state trooper you see who looks like they sewed the uniform on him? You know, every crease sharp and just right. Or some surfer dude." She squinted. "*Ex*-surfer dude."

He drank the last of the coffee and walked the empty mug to the sink. Took a soapy sponge to it, rinsed it, put it in the rack. Stood with his back to the window, the tidy curtains, the swing set in the backyard next door. Somebody built Henry a doghouse. Roger, maybe. Or Judy.

"You crapped out somewhere, didn't you?"

He couldn't help but smile at that.

"Yeah, I know you," she said, pointing the cigarette at him.

No you don't.

"Everybody's got a story," she added.

Some of us have more than one.

Judy came down wearing her company smock over a blouse, slacks and black rubber-soled shoes.

Bonnie said she'd take him to the train station. Smoke hung in the air.

"I don't know how to thank you, Sam," Judy said.

He stuck out his hand, but she went on her toes and kissed his cheek.

He needed a shower, but he wouldn't impose.

In the upstairs bathroom, he took off his shirt, hiding the pistol beneath it, and ran the hot water. Found a fresh facecloth in the cupboard. The soap smelled of a chemist's idea of a flowery field. No man lived here. If he'd wanted to shave, he'd have to do it with that pink disposable.

Steam coated the mirror over the sink as he wet his face and hair. He soaped the cloth and began to scrub the back of his neck, under his chin, his eyes closed. He worked a finger behind his ears—

He felt cool air enter the room.

He turned and there was Bonnie and she'd had the idea to take off her T-shirt and her bra and unbutton the top of her shorts, and she stood in the doorway, thumbs in her belt loops.

She came at him and kissed him on the mouth, stabbing at him with her tongue, and he tasted cigarettes. She reached between his legs and tugged at him.

He stepped back. Hot water splashed his arm.

She let her shorts fall to the floor and she was naked. She turned and bent over. Grabbing the towel rack, she offered herself to him. She said, "Come on. Come on, Sam. I'm ready."

He hadn't been with a woman since Louisville. He could do this and then he'd be gone. In time, he'd forget.

"Come on, Sam." Pleading, demanding. She slapped her butt. "Come on."

He shut off the water.

"No," he said.

She spun to face him.

She had butterflies tattooed on her sprawling breasts and he could see where her shorts pinched her pale skin.

He stared at her eyes. Rejection boiled to anger. She threw a punch. He caught it. He never stopped staring into her eyes.

With his free hand, he grabbed her under her chin, a gesture that was almost tender. If he dropped his grip 6 inches or so, he could cut off the air and he'd place her on the bath mat.

"Your husband," he said. "Three kids."

The way you treated your mother.

He let her go.

He tossed her the towel he'd laid on the sink.

He was going to say it: I don't know your sister. You can't take me from her.

But he wasn't cruel and he needed a ride.

CHAPTER 5

"You're some dumb son of a bitch, you know that?" said Bonnie at curbside in Milwaukee, leaning across the front seat. "You're thinking she's all that, but you're gonna find out. You'll find out."

He thanked her for the ride.

He didn't mention he'd seen a car driving slow on Judy Szarsynski's block, circling like it was scoping for the easiest mark. A black Cadillac DTS. Tinted windows. New, with Illinois plates.

Maybe it was Alvarado's brother, maybe it wasn't.

He found a phone booth in the train station and called the West Allis police. Asked for the patrol division's shift captain.

"I don't know if this matters," he began, "but I just saw a black Cadillac..."

He boarded the 11 o'clock to Union Station. Nestled in the quiet car and slept until the conductor woke him 90 minutes later.

Back in Chicago, he walked through chalky air to Clinton Street and the Blue Line, zigzagging through the lunchtime crowd.

His furnished room was over in Logan Square. A month's lease, as always, and never once did he stay the full 30 days.

He showered, he changed.

Outside, he looked this way, that way. Nobody.

Everything but the sneakers and belt went in the Dumpster.

Two hours' sleep. He showered again and shaved. He put on a blue blazer and walked off wearing the same brand of black jeans, the same white oxford, the shirt coming from the Chinese laundry with a paper strip across the chest.

To Staropolska's. Mushroom pierogi, potato cutlets with brown gravy, a cold brew. He used their pay phone. As he doubled back to the L, he was thinking it might've worked better with a suit, heading, as he was, to the Chicago Mercantile Exchange to see Taylor McHugh, whose card he found in Mary Louise's briefcase.

Or maybe not. Either way, one sentence would tell if he'd played it right.

The Blue Line to West Jackson. The Chicago Merc's art deco building, once the tallest in town. People were exiting, their day done. Swimming against the tide, he went to the desk and asked for McHugh. Security wanted his ID. He showed them an Indiana driver's license. John Bleak of Lebanon. He'd never been there and couldn't remember the last time he was in Indiana, but he knew the city was pronounced differently than the country between Israel and Syria. That detail alone usually got him through. As it did today.

He reached reception on the floor that housed the business development group.

"Taylor McHugh, please," he said, as glass doors sealed behind him.

The receptionist had 100 teeth, and each one of them sparkled like they'd been buffed by machine.

"Who shall I say—"

The badge stuck to his lapel told her the name he was using. But he said Mary Louise Szarsynski sent him.

The sentence.

McHugh appeared.

She wore a dark suit with gold buttons, a black scoop-neck blouse, and her gold choker matched her earrings and bracelets. Once a brunette, she was blond with streaks in various subtle shades. She carried a leather folio and the latest iPhone. Everything about her exuded speed and efficiency, like a guillotine's blade.

They shook hands.

She directed him to a woody conference room and gestured to a seat facing a wall of windows.

She settled on the other side of the long table, the city spread behind her.

"Mary Louise Szarsynski told you to see me," she said as she opened the folio and unclipped a thin gold pen. The top page of the legal pad was blank.

He said nothing as he stood and moved to the seat by the door.

McHugh turned. "And—?"

He said, "She has a mild concussion, contusions, a sprained ankle. She was lucky."

"A concussion? What happened?"

"Assaulted."

"When?"

"You were the last person she spoke to."

"Are you with the police?"

He said no. "You were the last person—"

"Is that relevant?"

He shrugged.

"And how can you possibly know if it's true?"

He didn't need much more than he had. According to her cell, Mary Louise called McHugh yesterday at 5:26 p.m. The business card she'd had in her briefcase was new. A press release on the website said McHugh had joined the CME a couple of years ago after its takeover of the New York Merc. Judy asked if her daughter had trouble in New York.

"She was your administrative assistant at the New York Mercantile Exchange," he said. "She came here to see you after hours. Then…" He punched his palm.

McHugh sat back toward the skyline. "Is she all right?"

"I am telling you a man tried to knock the face off her head." He stood.

"Mr. Bleak, excuse me," McHugh said. "What exactly is your purpose?"

He waited by the door, unable to resist the spectacular view. He could see the Hancock Observatory and all the way to Lincoln Park. Lake Michigan shimmered in the early evening sun.

She was steady. He hadn't knocked her off stride. He couldn't tell if she already knew her former secretary had been damaged and had run from the hospital. McHugh gave him nothing.

"Whatever you were up to, it failed," he said. "And now you've got CPD."

She stepped toward him, leaving the folio and iPhone on the table. "Mr. Bleak, I'm going to assure you there's been a misunderstanding," she said calmly. "You're going to tell me exactly what happened. And then we'll figure out where you've gone wrong."

"Ask the police to show you the photos. Her cheek, her eye. The back of her head."

He opened the door and made his way back to reception. He waited for the elevator to arrive. Three things might happen next, each with its own meaning. McHugh would catch up and ask him back inside. Security would appear. Or he'd turn in his name badge, sign out and blend into the crowd on La Salle.

On La Salle, he headed west, the L stop over on Quincy.

Walking tall, Taylor McHugh returned to her office, passing cubicles, the sound of clacking keyboards and muffled phone calls trailing her. She shut the door and went to her conference table. She opened her folio, pushing aside a tall vase filled with yellow and red baptisia. Arranging the names in a triangle, she wrote: John Bleak. Mary Louise. Francis Cherry. Boxing the names, she drew an arrow from Mary Louise to Cherry, from Cherry to Mary Louise. Another from Mary Louise to Bleak, from Bleak to Mary Louise. In the space between Cherry and Bleak, she drew a question mark.

On a separate page: John Bleak?

Mary Louise sent him.

Or did Francis Cherry?

She twirled her pen between her index and middle fingers.

Cherry.

Was John Bleak's appearance a veiled threat by Cherry?

John Bleak asked for nothing.

But he thinks I was involved in the attack.

Was I?

Mmmmm.

Cherry.

Why did Francis Cherry want to know if I'd heard from her? Why did he ask me to let him know if she called?

What does she know? What does she have?

She didn't say.

"Is there a job for me here, Taylor?"

"Are you relocating, Mary Louise?"

"I'm thinking about it. Maybe I'll move home. I don't know. New York is, it's, you know…"

"Come by for coffee. We'll chat."

Something. She has something.

What?

Cherry.

Opportunity.

Taylor McHugh sat back. She smiled.

Thank you, John Bleak.

Tonight he'd ride the Red Line. The White Sox were in town. He'd fall into the crowd going and coming. It'd be fine. No one would see him. No one would care if he was there. He didn't matter. Soon he'd be somewhere else. He knew how to live on the road. He left home for good at age 14.

Up high on the L, he passed through the Loop three times, and each time he saw the empty space in the garage where the rental car had been. Maybe it was in CPD's pound. Maybe Mary Louise Szarsynski retrieved it. Maybe she was on her way. Easy to hide in America if you kept your head down and your mouth shut, though yellowing bruises on a pretty face and an aching ankle might make it tough. You're a guy working in a filling station, diner, motel, nothing much ever happens, and someone asks you if you saw a young woman who fit that description. You remember. Sure, you say. She headed east. She headed west.

Or maybe she went to the cops and gave them the envelope. Told them everything. They ask about Fernando Alvarado, found down the hall from her hotel room. There was this guy. Sam. Tall guy; what's the word? Sinewy. Sandy hair. Weathered, kind of. He had a tiny scar near the corner of his right eye. It looks like a little teardrop.

Never saw him before, no.

Did he have something to do with all this?

Either way. The road, the cops. As long as he didn't have to stand by and watch somebody hit her in the face again. As long as nobody put her mother through another night like that.

As the train left the Garfield station heading south, his cell phone rang. He fluttered with hope. Pup. Finally.

When he said he didn't care what anybody thought? Not true.

"This is Mary Louise. Szarsynski. From, you know…"

"Hold on."

He stood and waded crablike through the crowd to the doors.

"Are you there?" she asked.

"Who gave you this number?"

"You called me this morning, remember?"

He did. She didn't answer.

"You told my mother your name is Sam."

It's not. "Listen—"

"They burned down her house."

"What?"

"They ransacked it and they burned it down."

"Your mother—"

"No one was hurt. Not even Henry."

The dog.

"A miracle," she said.

But the house was destroyed.

"Sam. My mother's house—" Her voice caught in her throat.

He looked around. No one was listening.

"Where are you?" he asked. He had his blazer folded over his arm. The forced air in the train failed to combat the night heat.

Ann Arbor, she told him. Michigan.

Yes, she had the car.

She didn't know what to do.

He got out at 63rd Street.

"Really. I don't know what to do."

"Call the cops."

"Sam—"

"Call them now."

"I can't."

Whoever sent Alvarado still wanted the envelope. Judy didn't have it. They needed to find Mary Louise.

They were desperate.

"Call the rental car company. Tell them you need it for a few more days."

"I could fly—"

"Don't show your ID unless you have to. Pay cash. Do you have money?"

"Money. Yes. Are they coming after me, Sam?"

"Keep moving," he replied.

Then he said, "Dump your phone. Buy a prepaid."

"Where do I go?" she asked.

"Someplace you've never been."

"Oh God."

"Taylor McHugh isn't your friend."

"Tay— How do you know Taylor?"

"Don't tell her where you are."

"Sam."

"Throw a dart at a map."

"Who are you?

"And then figure out if what's in that envelope is worth losing everything you've got."

She was silent. He wondered if she'd cut the connection. "Mary Louise?"

She said, "I'm going to call you."

"Don't call anyone."

He waited. Then he said, "All right?"

She said, "Tell me your real name."

He'd had so many names. "Mary Louise—"

"Tell me. I need to know." She sounded like a kid.

Without thinking, he said, "Nathaniel Hill. Now say good-bye."

She said, "Good-bye, Nathaniel Hill."

"Go," said Francis Cherry.

Ian Goldsworthy sat on the sofa, his back to Broad Street, quiet now as night settled. Every now and then, a police car siren screamed.

"Carlos Alvarado isn't returning calls."

Cherry was behind his desk. A solid-gold miniature gyroscope sat in the palm of his hand, a gift to Léon Foucault from Napoleon III. Cherry paid $114,000 for it. The Cite des Sciences et de l'Industrie in Paris was eager to display it for children and teens. They'd sent an emissary. Cherry kept it in his private bathroom.

"Why not?" Cherry asked.

"Because he knows he mucked it up."

"You're saying it's on him."

"Well…" Goldsworthy had spectacular silver hair that swooned over Spock-like ears, but a life of misadventure had added at least a decade of wear to his long, slack frame and skeletal face. "Yes. He had the assignment."

"But there are those who would say I gave you the assignment."

The Brit offered to protest.

To silence him, Cherry pointed with a finger of his free hand. "Did I or did I not?"

"You did," Goldsworthy conceded.

"But instead..."

"A degree of distance—"

"So you assumed you'd fuck it up."

"No, sir. But I thought it preferable—"

"Did you tell him to burn down the house?"

Goldsworthy said no.

"Did you think, when you told him to burn down the house—"

"Excuse me, sir, but I didn't tell him—"

"You gave him the address."

How did he know? "I'm sorry, but I said nothing about torching the house."

"So when your man was divinely inspired to burn down the house, do you think he considered, or did you consider, that the package — which is flammable, I might add — was inside?"

"Sir, if I may—"

"You farmed it out and the guy is burning down houses. And he calls me."

"There's no excuse," said Goldsworthy. It was the best he could do. Ex-MI6, the ruinous lifestyle that had damaged his body had done irreparable harm to his mind as well.

"If I recall, I said, 'Get on a plane, go downtown to the Merc, wait, follow, retrieve.' Could it have been any easier?"

"No—"

"The brother found her. No problem."

"I told him—"

"Now is not the time to claim credit."

Goldsworthy looked at his long fingers. "He did indeed. The brother found her. Right."

"Maybe you want to tell me why you felt you couldn't handle it yourself?"

Goldworthy withheld his reply. He'd yet to voice what he thought was obvious, at least to anyone who had known him in his prime in Mombassa, in Kinshasa, in Kashmir. He was no longer up to the task. The streets were beyond him now.

"Upon further review, sir, I—"

"Get her back," said Francis Cherry.

CHAPTER 6

He was leaving. Disappearing. He didn't want to be here. He was gone.

No he wasn't.

They burned Judy Szarsynski's house.

After leaving her daughter for dead in a parking garage.

Did you hear how frightened she sounded?

You are on the road alone, and someone is coming to kill you. Turn a corner, open a door, step for a moment through darkness. You hear something. Hello? Is somebody—? And then you're dead. You were and now you are not.

He went back to his room. He stripped to skin, and washed with soap and a hand towel. He put on a long-sleeved navy T-shirt, and he retrieved his sneakers from the windowsill. He removed the gun from the plastic bag he'd secured in the toilet tank.

He went into a bar on Pulaski and called intensive care. Fernando Alvarado was still there.

The L again, on, off.

Down into the hospital's underground garage. He couldn't locate the black Cadillac DTS with Illinois plates. He emerged and circled the neighborhood. The car was parked on Erie, a short walk from where he buried the gun the night before.

He rested against the planter, arms folded, ankles crossed. CPD passed twice. He was hidden by shadows. The moon was a dull sliver behind vapor clouds.

Here he comes. The man he saw driving in West Allis.

Carlos Alvarado.

A dark blue suit or maybe it was black, white shirt and necktie. Loafers so new their soles scratched the concrete as he walked. A steady, purposeful pace. A serious man. Deep in thought, his face knit tight, jaw clenched.

He sprang and drove a brutal uppercut deep into Alvarado's solar plexus.

Alvarado collapsed to his knees. He couldn't breathe. He heaved. He gulped for air.

Straddling the fallen man from behind, the man who sprang from the shadows put the muzzle of the pistol against Alvarado's neck.

"How does it end?" he asked.

Alvarado couldn't answer.

He pressed the muzzle deep into flesh.

Alvarado struggled to speak. But nothing came but a dry grunt.

"How does it end?"

"I don't know what you're talking about," Alvarado managed.

"Tell whoever sent you that she's not alone. Tell them you don't want to die for this."

He kicked Alvarado hard in the ribs. He kicked him again. Maybe a rib would puncture a lung.

He saw it: Judy called to the phone at work; Judy, your house is on fire. She finds everything gone. The drawings on the refrigerator. The wallpaper she'd chosen for the bath. Maybe she had a box of photographs on a shelf in the closet. A life gone to flames.

He spun him and stomped his face, driving his head against the concrete.

He went to a knee, grabbed Alvarado by the knot in his necktie and shoved the barrel of the gun into his slack mouth.

Alvarado was unconscious.

He let him go. Alvarado's head bounced on the sidewalk.

He kicked him again.

He used his own phone. Walking west, passing the hospital. Big town. A sweltering night, the windless city. Broad shoulders. Yes it is true, Sandburg wrote, I have seen the gunman kill and go free to kill again.

"Judy," he said.

"Sam?"

"The man who burned down your house is on East Erie between Fairbanks and McClurg."

"Sam, wait."

"Tell the police. Tell them to hurry."

He put the phone in his pocket.

He was done here. Chicago had memories now, connotations. It was the place where…

He crossed the glowing river twice. At Michigan and again at Adams, the phone buzzing in his pocket, callers dispatched to voice mail. The person he wanted to hear from never called. At Union Station, he stood staring at the board, the gun tucked against his spine. Trains. He could go anywhere. Nobody cared if he came or if he stayed away.

The man behind the ticket counter asked for ID. Anthony Faithful of Dallas, Oregon, and the man said he didn't know there was a Dallas in Oregon…

The bookstore was open.

Cherry patronized the same dozen restaurants in Manhattan. When his secretary's secretary called, a table was made available. An exquisite Bordeaux was served, at a price never less than $1,500 per bottle. He swilled it. Ordering it brought him the subservience he craved, not merely from the waitstaff but from the night's guest, usually an apparatchik three steps down on some firm's org chart, the kind of guy who overheard, who placed orders. Cherry tucked his napkin into his collar and kicked off his shoes. He ate the sour cream from the serving bowl, bacon bits by the handful like candy. Since he was hugely successful, he was considered amusing. The people who scorned him couldn't fathom how he survived. He had risen beyond talent, beyond good fortune, beyond savagery.

He had an apartment in Trump Tower on Fifth Avenue. The phone rang; Mr. Cherry's private line. Expecting Alvarado, Ian Goldsworthy ran to it. Yes, Ms. McHugh. He's not here, said Ian Goldsworthy. He cannot be reached, no. Of course I will tell him, Ms. McHugh.

She called the Wall Street Bath & Spa, and they pulled him out of a sauna full of Russians.

"I hate to be blindsided," Taylor McHugh began.

"You do. So what?"

"I need to know what you've done." She was at home now, barefoot, still in her suit, a glass of Sancerre in her hand. She looked down on the lake. The Ferris wheel spun on the Navy Pier. She'd made notes.

Cherry had a towel wrapped around his waist and paper shower shoes under his feet. He glistened. Considering his ruinous ways, he was remarkably fit. Rich and graceless, the Russians admired him, calling him comrade. They speculated and concluded his real name was Cherenkov. It wasn't.

"With Mary Louise," she said. "I need to know, Francis."

"How did your conversation go?"

"She was assaulted. A concussion. They brought her to the hospital."

"Send flowers."

"I can't. She's gone and she's not answering her cell," McHugh replied. "There's no answer at her mother's."

"Her mother's what?"

"House. Her mother's house."

A pile of charred wood and ashes. "What did she tell you?"

"I think we should clarify something, Francis. In the past, when we've—"

"Tedious," he said. "Make your point, then go away."

"This man—"

"What man?"

"The man who came to my office," she said. "He believes I was involved in what happened to Mary Louise."

"You are," Cherry said.

"Excuse me?"

"You taught her what she knows."

"He's talking about the assault, Francis."

"'The assault.' What? She was mugged?"

"A man came to see me."

"What man?"

"John Bleak."

John Bleak?

Cherry said, "Look, the other day you called to tell me your old admin was visiting you. I told you to tell her I said hello. Huh?"

"You set her up."

"Me. From New York. Hoo boy."

"Why are you after her?"

"If I am, it might be because she stole from me. From me, she stole, if that's what I'm saying. What she stole I want back."

"What is it?"

"Did you ask her?"

McHugh sighed. "Had you told me you wanted something from her—"

"I could swear I did. Didn't I? What an oversight."

Outside the sauna, the air conditioning in the corridor bore down on Cherry, removing the pink from his skin and sending him toward a chill.

"At any rate," he said, "she made a big mistake. A big mistake."

"How can I help?"

Cherry smiled. "No opportunity skates, huh?"

"I think you would concede there's a problem, Francis. Francis?"

Cherry passed the wireless handset to a towel boy and stepped back inside the sauna, dousing the hot rocks with a ladle of lukewarm water. Steam hissed, a cloud rose, he sat. Soon he returned to baby pink, a billion beads of sweat covering the top of his head. He closed his eyes. *Woodya-woodya nyoingy-nyoingy* Russian and heavily accented English careened off the wooden walls, and every now and then, a belly laugh, the sound of a meaty hand slapping damp skin.

It took him 34 hours to reach Salt Lake City on the California Zephyr. He could've booked a roomette and slept in comfort, but he stayed in coach and ate in the public dining car. He showered with liquid soap and tangerine-scented shampoo. A kid in pale dreadlocks and a hoop through her eyebrow, maybe she was 18, tried to chat him up, standing over him, leading with her hips and scent, but he kept his nose in one of the five books he read as they went west, killing 1,400 miles, killing Chicago. By the time he left the train and walked into the cool air in Pioneer Park, Chicago was in the deep past. Two days ago, two months ago, two years ago: all gone in the mist, something that happened once. He stared at the Wasatch Mountains, the Oquirrhs. The vista stunned him. It left him unguarded. He remembered his wife favored a brand of oatmeal soap; he saw the birthmark on her shoulder as he stroked her skin with a loofah glove, the hot shower water shooing the suds down along her back and legs.

He dug his fingernail into his earlobe until he acknowledged the pain. Long ago, not long ago, in Georgia's Chattahoochee Forest, he saw a flying squirrel leap from a tree, smack into another and tumble to the earth. The squirrel stood, shook his head, looked up at him. "What the hell happened?" the little beast seemed to think before darting off.

He decided he'd rent a car to find summer snow, to hold it in his hands.

He hung his head and started walking east toward the skyline, found a newspaper honor box, read the real-estate ads, circling the ones he favored with a pen from a bank that handed them out for free. Within the hour, he signed a 30-day lease. The city had a light rail system. The Sandy/Salt Lake Line.

He went to the mall for his oxfords, T-shirts, jeans, a new blue blazer and paperback novels. It was raining when he came outside. He put the gun in one of the shopping bags.

CHAPTER 7

Carlos Alvarado was treated at Northwestern Memorial. They padded his bruised ribs and recommended butterfly stitches to the wound on the back of his head. Alvarado said no and struggled into his shirt and jacket. Chicago police escorted him to look at Fernando, done up in valves and electrodes.

He rode a patrol car in a Vicodin haze. "Strange how you work with your victims," he said from inside Interrogation 2 at the precinct. He resented their treatment, but his singular sense of decorum remained in place. Throughout the interview, he stared at his face in the two-way mirror. That son of a bitch. He could see the outlines of a footprint on his cheek, though it wasn't there.

He'd done 20 months in Chino. Aggravated assault, the victim now fixed with a prosthetic jaw. "That was nine years ago. Another lifetime," Alvarado said. "So don't you confuse that man and me. I am a successful businessman, and respected."

The cop called him a legal loan shark. The Alvarado brothers ran a chain of bail bond agencies throughout southern California.

The other cop asked if he was chasing a runner.

"I am here to return my brother to our home. Dead or alive."

The two cops looked at each other. They heard the wind howl. They felt a chill on the back of their necks.

Says here you killed a man in prison.

"No. It does not."

You wormed out. Some other beaner took the fall.

A thousand-dollar suit. What's it mean, Mr. Alvarado?

"Fourteen hundred," Alvarado replied.

In Chino, Carlos Alvarado earned an MBA by mail. He scraped East LA off his skin a millimeter at a time. He worked vigorously to develop a personal code of conduct that rejected impulse and temper, teaching himself to project malevolence through inflection, terror through implication. He hadn't had so much as a shoving match in years. Now he was going to have to step up.

Cops let him go, declining his request for transportation.

At his hotel, he pissed blood. The painkillers wore off.

Turned out Salt Lake City's light rail system wasn't much. A little over 17 miles. After four days, he'd memorized the names of every stop. People began to look familiar. He took to wandering, falling into an ancient habit. First time he ran off he was eight and he stayed away for six weeks. The cops brought him back to the ranch. When they left, his father closed one eye, raised his old Remington rifle and pointed it at his only son.

Now he ended up over by the airport where the streets were named after aviators. Wiley Post, Billy Mitchell, Amelia Earhart. One-hundred-degree temperature at noon. Chilly after dark, the sky star-dotted and indigo blue. He had a cowboy steak, medium rare. The Tabernacle Choir rehearsed on Thursday nights. Every day at noon an organ recital. He met a woman. She shone like moonglow and had freckles everywhere. Pale green eyes. Her boots were handmade in El Paso. Her scent reminded him of the desert. Most men won't shut up, she said. But you're some other kind. Room service, Wiley? He declined. The point being, she said as she buttoned her blouse, I couldn't go through the whole routine again. But I sure do like the way you kiss.

He was thinking he'd head back north. The sun baked through his hair. His skin felt dry. Walking along, he found a doll's head, its eyes gouged out. When he picked it up, a tiny lizard leaped from the cavity and landed on his shirt. Thing stayed there for three miles. He gave it a name. The sky was out of reach. He was sitting in an oyster bar when his cell phone rang. Without thinking, he tugged it out of his pocket. A 414 area code.

"Sam?"

"Judy. Judy Szarsynski." He walked across terrazzo tile toward a black-and-white alcove.

"Sam?"

"I'm here," he said.

"Sam, I have to ask you something and I need you to tell me the truth."

It was flooding back now: the slim, chestnut-haired woman getting punched in the face in the parking garage; the man with the square-jaw beard in the hotel room; the iron; the Mercantile Exchange; a house on fire; Alvarado on Erie Street. The gun in Alvarado's mouth.

"Are you in California?"

I am not.

"Sam, did you send me money?"

I did not.

"Someone sent me money," she said. "I thought maybe it was you."

It was not.

"A FedEx package came to the school," Judy Szarsynski said. "Eleven thousand dollars is a lot of money, Sam."

He peered down the zinc bar where his dinner waited on ice, a frosty beer standing guard.

"Do you know someone named Henry M. Paulson Junior?"

He told her to look at the signature on the bills.

After a moment, she said, "The secretary of the treasury. Right."

"Judy—"

"The ZIP code is 90028. On the FedEx label."

"Hollywood."

"Is it my Mary Louise?"

Might be. Probably.

"The handwriting on the label doesn't look like hers."

"Judy, listen—"

"Have you heard from her?"

"Good-bye, Judy."

There was a time when it would've pained him to be considered rude. But now he didn't care what anybody thought. His time was his own. His life was his own. He never thought he'd settle down. He never thought he'd have anything they could take away.

For the second time, Alvarado headed north along 94, now in a steel-blue Buick, the road sun-drenched, trucks commanding the center lane. He was a patient driver. He settled in and kept it steady, looking at the green signs, drinking bottled water, the radio silent. He pulled into the Kenosha rest area, went into the men's room. The guy scrubbing the sinks saw him and backed out, bowing.

No blood. Finally.

Over brown linen slacks, he wore a yellow guayabera blousy enough to hide the padding around his damaged ribs. As he walked slowly back to the rental car, he stared at the rushing traffic on the highway, his teeth clenched. His eyes watered. As a boy, he punched a wall — his father was an ineffectual man; he would not stand tall — and fractured two knuckles and his scaphoid bone, an injury that did not cause as much pain as now radiated from the center of his torso. Each breath was torture. But the painkillers dulled his thinking. They made it difficult for him to manage his rage.

Soon he was back in West Allis.

He drove to the address Cherry's man Goldsworthy had given him the previous week and found a jagged skeletal frame and mounds of ashes. The seared-wood scent was almost gone, but mud puddles still scored the property. Once a family home, well tended, a source of pride. Now, rubbish ready for the Dumpster at the curb. A white patrol car from the city's fire department was in the driveway. Behind yellow tape slung between trees, men in uniform inspected the remains, circling, nodding.

Alvarado wondered who Cherry sent to set the fire. Maybe it was Goldsworthy himself. He wondered if he found what Cherry was looking for.

At the stop sign he reviewed the information he'd written down this morning in the hotel's business center, the first time he'd emerged from the room in two days. When he'd returned, a paper cup of takeout coffee in his hand, an enormous man, scar-faced with a huge head, was waiting. Alvarado had known the man's stepfather in Chino and had put up his bail three years ago, knowing full well he would lam — meaning the son would owe. The giant nodded timidly as he put down the colorful carton he'd held, releasing the plastic handle that had been lost in his grip. Alvarado brought the box inside his room, while his visitor retreated to the elevator, shivering in relief when the automatic doors sealed and Fernando wasn't inside, a gut-hook knife in his fist.

A dollhouse, according to the packaging. Assembly required. But in fact a sawed-off shotgun, an Italian model, and a box of shells. Alvarado then walked it through the lobby of the hotel and not a soul noticed. A wave of relief ensued. His first step back on the street was a success.

The giant had also provided a Smith & Wesson 910. Six hundred and fifty dollars out of the box. The shotgun was under the driver's seat, the pistol in the glove compartment. Both weapons were fully loaded.

He looked at it this way: he was filling in for his brother. It didn't mean he'd regressed. He was still the man he had become.

He'd decided to see if he could gut out Salt Lake City until the lease was about to expire. He had nowhere to be.

But he couldn't keep his mind occupied. Nothing he read pulled him in deep enough. He thought about buying an MP3 player, but music held memories so vivid it would be like time traveling. One day it rained like a son of a bitch and he slept for 23 hours. He couldn't find a Chinese laundry.

As Anthony Faithful, he rented a car. He decided he'd drive to Park City. He heard a couple in a bar talk about a pork sandwich they'd had up there. It'd come to that.

He was walking along Main Street, looking in shop windows, grateful for the chill in the air. There was a ranch about a half mile out of town in the Uintas. He hadn't been on horseback since he left home for good.

Staring at the hats in the window of a saddlery when he felt a tug on his elbow. "Your phone's ringing," said the young woman who had hazel eyes and skin the color of adobe.

He dug it out.

"Mr. Bleak, this is Taylor McHugh."

He cut the connection.

She called three more times. He looked at the number. Not from her phone at the Chicago Mercantile Exchange.

"Don't you get it?" he said as he walked back toward the rental car, the afternoon blown.

"Have you heard from Mary Louise?"

He tried to picture the streets coated with snow.

McHugh said, "I have to talk to you."

No you don't.

"Mary Louise Szarsynski isn't who you think."

He'd come back in winter. He'd bet the place was perfect when it snowed, the cold, clean air swooping down, faces chilled. He'd have that pork sandwich.

He turned off the phone. Why keep it? Who did he think was going to call?

You're failing as a cipher, pal.

Alvarado waited outside the shop. Melenchuk HVAC had two vans. Neither was driven by the man who beat him down and blindsided Fernando — the brother-in-law who visited the Szarsynski girl in the hospital. That man was very capable when coming out of the darkness. We will see how he does when the sun is shining.

The drivers were black men, lanky, agile on their feet. They wore the Melenchuk uniform with pride. Rarely were they gone for more than 90 minutes. They ate lunch together. Alvarado admired them. He wished he could find employees as dedicated and precise.

"Excuse me," he said. A little bell rang over the shop's front door. One man had already left, the other was closing up.

"You OK there?" the worker asked warily. The customer was making baby steps, his face taut in pain. Still, there was something about him, a spooky thing.

"My lungs," Alvarado explained as he reached the counter. "Emphysema."

The worker had removed his kelly jumpsuit. Some of the aura of professionalism had fled with it.

Alvarado introduced himself, laboring between sentences. "I am the insurance adjuster for the suspicious fire at the property belonging to Mr. Melenchuk's mother-in-law."

The man said, "All right…"

"I don't have his correct address," Alvarado continued. "I assume she's staying with them. Judith Szarsynski."

The man hesitated. "I'd better call him, get his OK."

"I don't want to make a thing of it. You know, it's kind of embarrassing. Just write it down and I'll be on my way."

"Won't take but a minute—"

Now Alvarado had the Smith & Wesson 910 pointed at him. "Write it down."

The man grabbed a bill of lading from a wire basket, turned it over and scribbled with a Melenchuk HVAC pen. Surrendering the paper, he stared dead ahead and groped for the billy club under the counter. He twitched.

Alvarado sent his brains against the back wall.

The recoil registering as shock through his body; Alvarado yowled, a sound so grotesque it seemed to linger as his senses returned.

CHAPTER 8

Cherry said, "I put it on you."

He was in his office in New York; she was in a conference room in Chicago. The mighty Hudson, and the green, you know, whatever the fuck river they had out there. Cherry insisted on video. He wanted to study her face.

In negotiations, even when they bordered on torture, every screw turned tight, midnight long gone and there's Taylor McHugh, composed, always on point, marble. Of course, she'd never negotiated over something like this. The way it was going, somebody was getting carted out in a body bag, maybe several bodies in several bags, or one body in several bags or whatever. So what? The cost of doing business. Are we children? And the envelope and whatever money remained would be returned to the safe where they belonged.

Though the money: Who gives a shit? Down here, in the shadow valleys off Broad Street, money sat in barrels at curbside. A never-ending supply. Worrying about losing money here would be like a Bedouin fretting over missing sand.

"That's what I decided," he said. "I put it on you."

"I wouldn't call that reasonable," she said.

She was wearing a bronze jacket over a white silk blouse. A gold necklace. He couldn't see her hands, but he knew the necklace matched the bracelet. Gold pen too. Every hair in place.

"I don't have to be reasonable," Cherry said. "I'm the aggrieved party."

"That's true," she allowed. "But your grievance—"

"—is with you. Like I said. You suggested I hire her. I did. Now this. You."

"Francis, why so testy today?"

"Don't play. Look at me, Taylor. I'm in the mood for games?"

McHugh said, "What would you like me to do? I ask you sincerely. What should I do?"

"Find her."

"Easier said than done."

"Think like her," Cherry said. "Every day for three years you spoke. What would she do?"

"Given the circumstances—"

"Would she stay in Chicago?"

McHugh said, "I think she may have been incentivized to leave Chicago."

She waited as Cherry sucked the filling out of a jelly doughnut, then licked the powdered sugar off his fingertips. Uncle Pennybags from the Monopoly game graced his yellow suspenders.

He said, "What about this guy she hired?"

"John Bleak? Noncooperative."

"Who is he?"

"I have no information other than a phone number her mother gave me. It's a cell. He could be anywhere."

"Give me the number."

"I've taken it upon myself to rectify this."

"You don't want to give me the number?"

"I'd rather not spend the rest of my career in debt to you," she said with the shade of a smile.

Cherry stared. Given McHugh had gobbled up at least four million off investments he made on her behalf as payback for leaking to him, she was already in his debt. Incredible that she didn't see it that way.

He said, "Because if you give me the number, Taylor, GPS technology puts me in the guy's lap, and then maybe somebody takes off his head, drops it on a platter, nice and centered, and says, 'Here's your muscle, Mary Louise.'"

"To coin a phrase," he added.

"Of course."

"Or not."

He leaned on his elbows, drawing closer to the camera.

"One week. Taylor."

"I'll report back in one week," McHugh replied.

"You'll find Mary Louise in one week."

"When I report to you, I intend to be able to tell you where she is."

"Taylor…" Cherry warned, pointing halfway across the country.

"Francis—"

"Whatever you're thinking — no. Don't."

Cherry stood, his midsection and groin filling the screen.

"One week," he said, rapping a knuckle on the desk as he began to walk away.

Then he returned, leaned over and stared into the camera.

"One week."

Alvarado pulled up outside the address he was given, easing up the block a bit. Outside the house, the man's bloated, tattooed wife sucked a cigarette, let her sausagey fingers fall from her lips. She blew smoke toward the evening sky and sucked again, pacing the lawn like she was holding back tears. She looked like she'd been crying for days.

He was watching through the rearview mirror. Kids played with a collie in the backyard of the pale-blue house. All three, they were fat like their mother. They didn't resemble their tall, sandy-haired father, who Alvarado had seen as he drove by the Szarsynski home last week, who that hefty woman led to the car, steam coming out of her ears. No, they didn't resemble that man, that very same man who kicked his head and cracked his ribs, who left Fernando for dead. Melenchuk, though Goldsworthy said he went by the name John Bleak when he worked for this Mary Louise Szarsynski.

The fence around the backyard had a gate, and a woman he assumed to be Judy Szarsynski came out. She was dressed neatly; even with a dish towel in her hand, she seemed correct. A grandmother in a baby-blue sweater. The smoker, though, with an obscenity on her T-shirt, the washed-out butterfly tattoo, those Michelin Man thighs…

He watched. A few words were exchanged. The mother dropped her hand on her daughter's arm. The daughter listened, her bottom lip quivering. A hug. The daughter hung on, clinging. Now she was sobbing.

He could hear her cries in the car, though the windows were sealed tight, the cool air dissipating quickly.

The kids came to the fence. A little bit frightened, they looked at each other.

He didn't know much about small towns in Wisconsin, but Alvarado figured if there's crying in the street, soon neighbors would appear. He could wait no longer. He reached under the seat for the shotgun.

The daughter stepped back. She flicked her cigarette toward the curb. Angry, again.

Alvarado was out of the car, the engine running. The driver's-side door hung open behind him. He moved mechanically, minus style, his teeth grit.

He cupped the muzzle of the shotgun in his hand, the barrel hidden behind his arm, extra shells in his pocket. After he exploded Melenchuk's face and head, he was going to have to reload and kill the rest of them too. Right there, in the evening sun.

The front door of the house opened and out stepped a man who weighed maybe 300 pounds, his faded denim shirt open, a T-shirt straining underneath. He wore shorts too, had gray knees and was barefoot. Hand on the wooden rail, he lumbered down the buckling steps.

"Bonnie. Honey."

Alvarado stopped.

Hold on. This was not the tall, sandy-haired man who attacked him. This was not the man he intended to kill.

"Bonnie, now..." the man said, leading with patience and sympathy. "Bonnie..."

Reaching his wife, Melenchuk waved to comfort the kids. He'd resolved to hold this thing together. A mistake had been made. An accident.

Alvarado was walking again, each step jarring him down to the blood cells.

Judy Szarsynski turned and looked directly at Alvarado. "Mr. Bollinger?" she said as he approached.

Alvarado drew a breath through his teeth.

"Are you Mr. Bollinger from the state fire marshal's?"

The kids were looking at him too.

Suddenly, Bonnie Melenchuk shouted, "I did it. All right? I dumped my butts and ashes in the trash, and they caught fire. I did it. Me." She thumped her chest. "It was me. *I* burned down the fuckin' house. Me."

Alvarado stopped. Melenchuk lumbered, his hand extended, an awkward smile, his huge head tilted. "Mr. Bollinger..."

A siren in the distance was drawing closer.

Melenchuk looked past Alvarado.

A police car squealed around the corner, fishtailing along the street.

Alvarado spun. Now he had the shotgun pressed tight against his outer thigh. Though the pain was unbearable, he hurried back toward the blue Buick, ready to fire if the cops called to him.

The police car shot by. It screeched to a stop in front of the Melenchuk house.

Alvarado sat behind the wheel of the Buick and tucked the shotgun under the seat.

In the rearview, he saw two cops jump from the patrol car and hurry toward the family.

As a sergeant spoke, Melenchuk clasped his head in anguish. His wife groped to comfort him as his mother-in-law covered her mouth in shock, the dish towel dropping to the lawn.

Gasping in pain, Alvarado white-knuckled the steering wheel as he drove away.

A good day's sleep, then another, and he was moving again, his mind focused only on the moment. He went; he did. The art galleries at Ninth and Ninth, the Victorians on the avenues. He was hoping to see the first Kentucky Fried Chicken stand, but the building had been torn down. He'd never heard the word "malacology" in his life, so he went to the Natural History Museum of Utah to look at ancient mollusks. Memories were winning, marching through the mist. Over by the Little America Hotel, he got a straight-razor shave and a haircut.

Soon the weight of deliberate ignorance wore him down. It had happened before. The subconscious mind demands attention. Along 202 to the Great Salt Lake, he thought for a moment that his wife was in the passenger seat, a ghost along for the ride. He caught a whiff of her perfume as he reached for her hand.

On the ride back, the lake's sulfur stench lingered, despite the open windows. When he filled the tank, he bought an air freshener, looped it around the mirror. "Been to the lake?" asked the guy who washed his windows. "You didn't go in, did you?"

Defeated, he walked toward the Amtrak station, his blue blazer over his arm, a paperback book tucked in his back pocket. The snow-capped mountains were invisible to him now, but he saw the birds perched in a row on overhead wires.

He stopped when his phone vibrated in his pocket. He never liked that sensation. It meant someone had texted. The written word had heft and could be meaningful. Hope was a problem more debilitating than illusion.

Pls listen to voicemail. PLS!

Taylor McHugh.

He stuffed the phone away, and told himself he wasn't disappointed. Told himself he felt nothing.

He had beaten himself down to zero, but Mary Louise Szarsynski had brought him back. He didn't like it. She was now part of the conspiracy that kept him from disappearing. He wanted to stay lost.

Pioneer Park. He sat on a bench, then decided to sit on the grass. Ran his fingers through the blades, picked a few, tossed them high to let them blow in the gentle wind.

Cherry called. Not Goldsworthy, him with that bullshit British accent. Francis Cherry.

Alvarado was in his hotel room, naked except for his boxer shorts. His ribs were ringed with yellow-purple bruises. In the mirror, he saw flab where he once stretched tight. In Chino, he did a thousand sit-ups a day. He could bench press 400 pounds, no problem. Now he typed 30 words a minute. He knew the California Insurance Code. He took accountants to lunch.

"Where have you been?" Cherry said.

Room service delivered dinner and with it, a bottle of *añejo* tequila. Alvarado had toasted his brother with the first glass.

With the second, he toasted the man he killed in West Allis. The first man he'd put down in a decade.

"Say again, Cherry."

"Where. Have. You. Been?"

"Oh, Cherry. You don't want to know."

The third glass, and the fourth and fifth, might allow him to forget the mistakes he'd made today.

"Are you drunk, Carlos?"

"A girl. A package. But you say nothing about a bodyguard."

"What bodyguard? John Bleak?"

"I will find this man," Alvarado said. "I will kill this man."

"You? Goldsworthy said you did the books."

Alvarado let woody tequila run along the back of his throat. "Yes and no, Cherry. I am responsible for the entire enterprise, and let me assure you that it is a very great success."

"Yeah, OK, good. Make sure I know when you're going public." Cherry was in a private room at a steakhouse on Exchange Place, the gigantic Stars and Stripes on the facade of the New York Stock Exchange in full view. He'd sent his guest, a junior trader at a bank based in Luxembourg, to the men's room. "Tell me about Bleak. You've seen him?"

Alvarado had seen men like Bleak his entire life. Tall, their hair turned golden by the sun, they walked with ease, long strides, these beautiful blue-eyed California men, honey coating their lips. They believed they would never have to prove themselves. They could not conceive that they would ever be tested.

"A bum," Alvarado said. "A Northern California ranch-hand bum."

"'A ranch-hand bum.' Hoo boy. Time you put away the bottle, Carlos."

"I won't toast that son of a bitch," Alvarado said as he refilled the glass. On the tray were the remnants of a T-bone steak he had eaten. Every bite rattled his rib cage; chewing caused searing agony. Acknowledging his return to a primal state, however temporary, he ate the meal with his hands, gnawing the blood-red meat down to the bone.

"Don't obsess," Cherry said. "I'm not laying out for revenge." If Cherry wanted somebody dead, he'd have sent Goldsworthy.

"Revenge would be a fractured skull, a coma. Or cracked ribs. This is not mere revenge."

Cherry rubbed the bridge of his nose. His guest was waiting beyond the room's frosted glass, too intimidated to risk returning before he beckoned. "Just go find the girl."

Alvarado said, "I need a private plane."

Cherry laughed. "You do, do you?"

"I'm taking Fernando back to Los Angeles. He can't fly commercial. It's too dangerous."

"He's awake?"

"He's awake," Alvarado confirmed. "They have given him medication to prevent seizures. Everything is precarious."

"And this is my problem *how*?"

"I stay here until Fernando flies home."

Cherry wasn't convinced Szarsynski had actually left Chicago. He reasoned that she wasn't clever. She'd lucked into the haul and didn't know what she had. If she did, she didn't understand the value. If McHugh called to say she found her, having Alvarado at hand might be all right.

"I have to think about this," Cherry said.

"One or two more days of observation, and then Fernando is ready to go home."

"We'll talk tomorrow. Stay put."

Tomorrow, Alvarado thought as he cradled the phone. What kind of man will I have to be tomorrow?

CHAPTER 9

He intended to move on to Denver. Denver. Why not? He hadn't been there for decades, back when he was looking for something better, before New York, before Pup was born and before it all went to hell. Mountain air, morning sun, cooling afternoon thunderstorms. A light rail system. A hike across the Front Range until he saw pink veins in the granite of Pikes Peak. Then along the South Platte, and he wouldn't meet a soul. It didn't matter if he was there or not. He meant nothing to nature. The 4:35 a.m. California Zephyr out of Salt Lake City arrived at 7:45 p.m. He'd sleep all day.

One, please.

The guy didn't ask for ID. You'd be surprised how often that happened.

Now he had a night to kill. Seated on the station's front steps, he finished the paperback shortly after midnight. He studied the diamonds in the sky.

He washed at the men's room sink, the soap coming out like shaving cream. He scrubbed with paper towels.

He stared at the rust on the tracks, this way and that. Supermarkets had book aisles. Convenience stores had a few books on a rack. He had four hours to roam. But he didn't want to go back. Salt Lake City. That was then, this is now.

In the empty terminal, he found a discarded copy of USA Today, its sports section missing. He didn't look at newspapers for the same reason he avoided the Net. They were about somebody's idea of what was valuable and necessary to know. They were about the past too. He didn't need anybody to tell him about the past and what it meant. The last thing he'd do is Google his own name.

He went back outside. He heard cars in the distance. Maybe the train coming for him was in Nevada by now.

He flapped open the newspaper. "Across the USA," 50 little summaries. Life in tiny paragraphs. He read every one, finally arriving at Wisconsin.

> **West Allis**: Police continue to search for the killer of 34-year-old Kwame Green, a technician at Melenchuk Heating, Ventilation and Air Conditioning. According to owner Roger Melenchuk, Mr. Green, a father of four, was shot during an attempted robbery at the company's offices here. The police are canvassing for witnesses to the incident.

He remembered the number for the West Allis police, but he didn't use it right away. He had been in West Allis and he was carrying. He had to think this thing through. He'd told the cops about a black Cadillac rental with Illinois plates circling the neighborhood. Now a home on the block was ashes and rubble. Judy Szarsynski would explain: my daughter was assaulted. Look at a man in intensive care down in Chicago. Alvarado. He has a brother. He's terrorizing my family.

He remembered McHugh's text.

Summoning her voice message, he put his phone to his ear.

A man's voice.

"Because if you give me the number, Taylor, GPS technology puts me in the guy's lap, and then maybe somebody takes off his head, drops it on a platter, nice and centered, and says, 'Here's your muscle, Mary Louise.'"

Then Taylor McHugh said, "Now you know the kind of man we're dealing with, Mr. Bleak. But tell me where Mary Louise is and I'll help her. I give you my word. I've been pulled into this too. I—"

Delete.

He scrolled through the phone calls he'd made and received until he found McHugh's cell number. She answered, groggy. But, clearing her throat, she said, "Mr. Bleak, I'm so glad—"

"Hollywood. She's in Hollywood."

"Hollywood, California?"

"He'd shoot a father of four."

"I'm sorry?"

"The kind of man we're dealing with."

He heard it. He'd said "we."

Been a good long while since he was one of "we."

They picked up Carlos Alvarado at his hotel.

He treated it like they said "West, Alice."

"Who is Alice West?" he asked. His head pounded so badly he almost forgot about his aching ribs.

Back in the box. Different cops. A guy from the Wisconsin state police too. A serious suit.

Alvarado limped to remind them he'd been injured.

Judy Szarsynski was looking through the two-way mirror. "That's him."

Bonnie Melenchuk agreed.

"Who is this Bollinger?" Alvarado said. "I don't know this Bollinger."

Mirandized.

"A man attacked my brother. The same man attacked me."

He was reminded that he had claimed he hadn't seen the man who snuck up on him, knocked him down, cracked his ribs.

"I understand you think my brother was involved in an incident with this woman. I don't know her name. My brother did nothing. He is a victim. I am a victim. All right, yes. West Allis. I heard a rumor at the hospital. People talk. It's true. I wanted to see her and explain. My brother, he was in a coma. He assaulted no one. I would ask this woman to look at my brother. Come and look at him."

Round and round. Fernando Alvarado assaulted no one but he was found in an alcove near Ms. Szarsynski's hotel room.

"Perhaps you would show me the courtesy of explaining what it is you think I did in West Allis?"

A nine to the front head.

Alvarado drew up. "This is the second time you have accused me of the ultimate crime."

The ultimate crime. What bullshit. Yet he sold it. The guy was ice despite the hangover. The state cop narrowed his eyes in admiration.

"I don't need to kill anyone. I am a businessman."

"Blah blah," said a Chicago cop, making his hand yap like a sock puppet. "Blah. Blah."

Alvarado kinked his neck. He stared. "I tell you: bring me the woman and she will know Fernando did nothing. Bring her to me."

In the hall, Bonnie Melenchuk said, "Holy shit…"

Wide-eyed, Judy Szarsynski stumbled as she retreated. She propped against the back wall.

"Ah. You don't react. So you know. You have nothing. Maybe you find that *cabron* who did Fernando and me and there is the man you need."

She was born in Buttonwillow and her father still worked in Bakersfield, but Taylor McHugh told everyone she was from Montecito, so in a sense, she was going home. O'Hare to LAX. She set up in a boutique hotel in West Hollywood. If it went like it should, Cherry was paying. Gardenias floated in a bowl on the nightstand.

She was at the rooftop pool, slathered in SPF 30. Sunglasses, her midriff bare. If she'd known, she would've been waxed. The water cooler was filled with lemonade. She compartmentalized. One hour of pure indulgence. It would last for weeks.

She called Cherry's office. Unavailable. She called his cell. Goldsworthy answered. McHugh knew he'd been drummed out of the Secret Intelligence Service.

"It's Taylor," she began. "Mary Louise is in Hollywood."

Cherry was on the Lower East Side, watching schoolyard b-ball, college-aged kids, a league of some sort, uniforms with press-on plastic numbers. Scorching, the sun parked over Houston Street melted the asphalt. The cop waving traffic through construction had sweat rings down to her hips. Summer in the city. On the court, the Jews were kicking the shit out of the black guys. The Jews were disciplined — set plays, never fewer than three passes.

They defended. The black guys couldn't wait to throw it up. They'd bounce it off the top of their heads, shoot it out of their asses. And a few were out of shape, all roly-poly and jiggling. Two old black guys sat on the next bench. "Too many hash browns," said one guy. The other guy cackled. "Hash browns" and they laughed, slapping their bony thighs.

America, Cherry thought. A black president and Jews who can ball. He was eating hot potato knishes out of a paper bag. Yonah Schimmel. Delicious. Unbelievable. Worth the lunch-hour limo ride from Wall Street. From under the shade trees, the Hasidim who watched the game nodded respectfully. They thought Cherry was a Jew, his birth name Cherkin or some such, a dealmaker, shrewd, a big *macher*. Not so. No, he was a *macher*, sure, but not a Jew. If they looked close, they would see he'd squirted ketchup on the knishes.

"Mary Louise is in Hollywood," said McHugh, when the call was forwarded.

Cherry suppressed a smile. Am I the luckiest fuck in the world or what? "Hooray for Hollywood," he replied.

"I'm nearby. Los Angeles," she added. She sipped lemonade through a straw.

"You are? Tell me where, Taylor. I should send a certain something your way."

She gave him the name of the hotel, knowing he would track her down if she didn't. "I have a proposal for you," she said.

Of course.

"Let's see if I can conclude your negotiations without further incident."

Cherry pondered all angles. "OK," he said finally.

OK? Really? "Tell me she won't be hurt if I bring her in."

"She won't be hurt if you bring her in."

"I give weight to your word, Mr. Cherry," she said.

Hold on. The black team was on an 8–0 run. Backs against the wall, they locked in. Hash browns were setting picks like concrete roadblocks, and the loping guys had turned into panthers. The Jews were looking for a lawyer.

"You get a fresh week," he told her. "Seven days."

"Make it ten." A boy in tennis whites approached with her avocado salad. "I may visit my family."

Enjoy Buttonwillow, thought Cherry.

A fistful of change at the newsstand, and then he stepped onto Wynkoop Street. "GPS technology puts me in the guy's lap." Bright lights a few blocks away. He walked over to Coors Field. A public-address announcer. Forty thousand people cheering. Baseball. He was going to buy a ticket, use a pay phone inside. But no. They'd hear the crowd. They, the opposite of we.

He found one near a parking lot on Wazee. Turned around to look at the Rocky Mountains. The pistol was in his jacket pocket.

Judy Szarsynski jumped in. "Sam. Have you heard from Mary Louise? I've been calling and calling…"

"Tell me about Kwame Green."

"How do—?"

The newspaper.

Green worked for her son-in-law. He played the organ at the black church. The kind of guy who couldn't be spared. He took the neighbors' kids ice-skating, waving his arms as he tried to balance, everyone sharing a laugh. "You know the way kids laugh, Sam."

Ah, Jesus, he thought. Sure I do.

He was hungry. He was tired too. He didn't sleep much on the train. A woman napped across the aisle. He lifted her book and read it before she awoke. He borrowed another from a conductor who boarded in Granby.

"Carlos Alvarado burns down your house. Now this," he said, musing without thinking.

"My house? Sam, no, Bonnie did that. It was an accident. Her cigarettes, you know. The trash, the curtains… But, no, Sam."

He looked at his sneakers. He looked at the sky.

"Sam?"

The girl lied.

"But the police think he shot Kwame," Judy Szarsynski said. "They brought him in for questioning and all. But they had to let him go."

One brother wallops Mary Louise. The other kills a man who works for her brother-in-law.

"You know, Sam, if it was you who, you know, with his brother in the hotel and then him on the street…"

I know. He's coming. He has to. He's been told to drop my head on a platter.

"What's it all about, Sam?

He said, "You save the FedEx envelope the money came in?"

"I think so. Why?"

"Give me the tracking number."

Shortly before midnight, a Cessna Mustang arrived at DuPage in West Chicago. The Alvarado brothers were waiting. Fernando was so doped he rag-dolled, but Carlos helped him up the airstairs, the co-pilot holding an umbrella and carrying their bags.

"Anything I can help you with, sir?" the co-pilot said once they were sheltered in the cabin.

"Turn back time," Carlos Alvarado replied, thinking it wasn't long ago that Fernando was on the job and a citizen who worked HVAC in West Allis was still alive.

"Let's fly backward," the co-pilot joked.

Carlos stared a hole in his face.

Back at the hotel, Carlos had showered his brother, scrubbing off the hospital scent. He'd trimmed his beard, combed his hair, staring at the bruise on the side of his face. He'd brought him a change of clothes — a sienna short-sleeve turtleneck, cream slacks, huaraches. In the stark bathroom light, Fernando looked pretty close to himself, his biceps pulsing despite the stretch in bed. But he was taking too long to reboot. The last thing Fernando remembered was leaving Alvarado Brothers Bail Bonds HQ on his way somewhere. "July?" he asked now. At least he remembered his name and, prompted, that he killed their crack-addled mother when she took a skillet to their baby sister. He was 14 then. "Carlos," he sighed. He accepted his brother's embrace.

Now Carlos strapped Fernando into his seat.

Cherry said to call when his ass met buttery leather.

"I hope it's up to your standards," Cherry said. He was home. A silk robe, the 38th floor. He could see yellow taxis racing through Central Park. Edith was the young woman's name.

The least you could do, Carlos Alvarado thought. He was looking at Fernando, whose oval eyes pinwheeled in his head.

"She's in Hollywood. Mary Louise," Cherry explained. "I'd bet she's never been there before."

Meaning scout Grauman's, the Paramount gate, Forest Lawn, the Walk of Fame…

"Plus there's a woman you should know," he added, giving Carlos the name of McHugh's West Hollywood hotel.

"These women will deliver him to me," Alvarado said.

"Undoubtedly," Cherry replied. "Hey. How's your brother?" He tried to make it sound like he gave a shit. Edith was parading naked in high heels, flashing 57th Street from above. She had a master's in English lit from Columbia, and legs. Hoo boy. There goes five Gs, and well worth it.

"My brother," Alvarado replied. "My brother is a man. He cannot be stopped."

A string of spittle hung from Fernando's lower lip.

Outside, the rain picked up and crossed the runway in sheets. The Cessna would have to burst through storm clouds on its way to Fullerton.

He simmered, he stewed. He worked the phones. He walked the Denver night, crossing Colfax and ending up at Civic Center Park. There were cops everywhere so he kept moving, passing the mint, the amphitheater, a municipal building, the state capitol with its golden dome. He tried to remember how many golden domes he'd seen.

He had a doughnut and coffee. He couldn't shake it. Mary Louise Szarsynski had lied about the fire, about her mother's home burning down to the ground. Why bother? Couldn't she tell he was passing through? Didn't she learn a damned thing in New York? You walk the streets, you look, you think, she's leaving, she's staying. He's counting the days, he's talking to a realtor. That one sitting on the curb, his head in his hands, a crack in his shoe leather? He should've never come.

Soon, the municipal workers dribbled in. First the uniforms, maintenance, cafeteria staff, the security day shift. Then the baggy suits. Then town cars and limos. The library opened. He read, he used the pay phone. He went to a convenience store and bought a travel kit. He shaved at the library sink, washed behind his ears. His blazer needed steam cleaning, a press. Six new shirts. Six, not five, not three.

She called. From a thousand miles away, he could smell the bougainvillea and lemon trees.

Mary Louise Szarsynski said, "Why did you lie to me? Your name isn't—"

"Vine, off Sunset." He told her the exact address and the time she was at the store to send the FedEx package back home.

She said, "You know, I believed you."

"You returned the car at Detroit Metro. Flew Spirit to LAX."

"Are you trailing me?"

He knew the name of her rental car company and told the Detroit office he was an agent calling from O'Hare. A missing vehicle. Spirit was a guess: only two airlines flew direct from Detroit Metro to LAX. If she had enough money to give away $11,000, she was flying direct.

She said, "I've been trying to reach you."

She had implicated him in the murder of Kwame Green. He knew what happened: when Alvarado was circling the neighborhood, he saw him with Bonnie. He assumed he was Melenchuk, her husband. He wanted revenge for his brother and the smackdown on Erie Street. Maybe he still wanted what was in the envelope. But he wanted the guy who blew his play.

The guy on McHugh's phone had called him "Mary Louise's muscle." They thought he was working for her.

"I called, but you won't answer," she said.

"You knew he didn't burn your mother's house."

"You lied too. Your name isn't Nathaniel Hill."

"How much is left in the envelope? You're out at least fifteen thousand."

"I had to shake you up."

He was sitting in the sun on a bench outside the library, a paper shopping bag at his side. Six white shirts and a gun.

She said, "I know your real name. Would you like to know how I know?"

"The people you put at risk."

"I'm in Westwood."

He stopped.

"There's a coffee shop not far from the Fox Theater on Broxton. Do you know it?"

He stood.

"I'm looking at it," she said. "UCLA students are over there."

He could see it, yes.

"There's a girl. She just turned nineteen. She's studying at the School of Theater, Film and Television."

He was walking along Broadway, away from the library. The shopping bag was back on the bench. He had the gun in his hand.

"She's already sold a script. I read that they gave her a lot of money."

Yes. True. That was Pup's deal with Koons and the agency. I write the treatment or let's not sell. Koons learned what Pup's mother and father already knew: once she made up her mind, her mind was made. Advice was background noise.

"This girl, she looks like you, Sam. Her hair's a little darker, but she's tall like you, and the sad eyes and—"

"What do you want?"

"Nathaniel Hill. That's her main character's name. The star, I guess. A vigilante. Some kind of damaged hero."

He was standing on the corner at 13th Avenue, the gun in plain sight.

"They're coming after me, Sam, and I'm alone."

CHAPTER 10

It had been a long flight for Carlos Alvarado, who boarded thinking, Oh, we're going to get that son of a bitch, Fernando. Don't worry. Me and you, we're going to pull out his tongue, throw it down at his feet and then we'll let the good times roll, believe me.

As the plane cleared weather and leveled off, he allowed his mind a picture of his brother standing tall, reporting in, making it work, the thing done, signing off, clock punched, hands washed. What's next, bro?

But Carlos could not sustain hope. Sitting across from him was a puppet with no one holding the strings. A man unplugged. Every now and then, Fernando emitted a dry sob from deep in his throat.

"Fernando?" Carlos thought his brother might speak, maybe offer some acknowledgment of the situation.

His chin on his chest, Fernando opened his eyes to look around slowly, uncertain where and who he was.

So by the time Cherry's jet began its descent, Carlos had been sunk by an emptiness as vast as the dark sky above the clouds. He withdrew to consider whether Fernando could return in any usable form. He needed an ally in this battle, someone as reliable as Fernando, who you told what to do and he did it, no fuss, no muss.

The Alvarados had been seriously compromised, courtesy of the muscle that Cherry or Goldsworthy never mentioned.

Forlorn and fatigued, Carlos Alvarado shook his head in dismay.

The Mustang landed with a bounce, jarring its two passengers and disturbing the starry calm. His ribs screaming, Carlos leaned over and tapped his brother on the thigh.

The driver from the car service, stupid black beanbag hat, held a sign. "ALRAVADO," it read.

"Are you retarded?" Carlos asked.

Me? thought the driver as he glanced at Fernando the daffodil.

Soon, they were heading north on I-5, passing under well-lit highway signs for Disneyland and Knott's Berry Farm. Fernando lolled soup-brained against the window, ogling the green-cheese moon.

Carlos had decided to put his brother up at his house, a gated Spanish-colonial-style one-story off Bundy, just south of Brentwood. He called their sister and told her to pick up some adult diapers on the ride over.

"You know," Carlos said to the driver, "if we came into Santa Monica Airport, we could have walked home."

"You're right, sir." He was new to the job. The dispatcher told him Carlos Alvarado was some kind of death merchant, a guy who could glare you into the grave. The driver saw an aging businessman fretting over a lump who'd taken a bad beat-down and came away minus parts.

He arrived at LAX a little after 10 p.m. He hated like hell to lose the gun, but he knew he could buy another in Orange County easy enough. He'd tried to read on the plane, but couldn't. Memories. The inevitability of all this. He wasn't sure if the flight took three minutes or three years.

He rented a car and drove toward the condo his father-in-law owned on Hilgard near the UCLA campus, but pulled over before he left Wilshire. He needed to pay attention, to be alert to reality. He needed to locate Pup without letting her see him. If he dropped in on the coffee shop off Broxton where Mary Louise Szarsynski saw her, Pup would ignore him. If he walked the campus and set up outside Melnitz Hall, she'd call security. If he said, Pup, hide, she would walk in sunlight.

She blamed him. Her thinking had calcified; she needed a villain. She had the facts wrong, but she was right. It had been his fault, though not in the way she thought. Only he knew what had happened.

Trying to win her back after Appleyard, Washington, made it worse. Apathy turned to acrimony, grief to anger. It no longer mattered that he hurt too. Go away, Pup said. Really. Just go away.

He drove back toward LAX and rented a room, telling the hotel desk clerk to keep it open-ended. Then he got back in the car and drove, trying to get lost on serpentine roads in the hills, entering on Topanga, exiting hours later east of the 101. He had breakfast at a roadside taco stand. He bought six shirts and a toiletry kit. He washed and shaved at a sink in the farmers market.

Now it was lunchtime. He got back in the car and drove over to Century City. He studied his tired eyes in the rearview, and after tossing the keys to the valet, slipped into his blazer, the one he bought in Salt Lake City. He tugged the lapels until it sat right.

The restaurant was filthy with executives and agents in silk suits. He recognized a few actors, but he didn't see who he was looking for. "Can I help you?" asked a young hostess who sparkled beyond possibility. He gave a name. He's on the terrace, he was told. She offered to escort him, but he held up his hand. Thank you.

Then he was back out in the sun. Koons saw him. Surprised, but he recovered. Then the agent frowned and was still frowning as he stood, gesturing to his companion to hold that thought.

"She won't see you," Koons said, looking up.

The man who had spent the night trying to outrun himself stuck out his hand. He said, "Michael."

What the hell. Michael Koons hugged him to his tiny frame, his head at his visitor's chest.

"But Isabel won't see you," he repeated as he retreated. "You know that."

He nodded. "How is she?"

"I can't say."

"You can't?"

"You know how it is."

His daughter's agent placed a hand on his elbow and walked him away from the crowded tables toward the busboy's stand.

"If she sees me talking to you…"

He hung his head. He was beyond humiliation. Everything had been misunderstood. There was no defense.

"There's a problem, Michael."

"She won't fold. She's absolutely—"

"Someone may approach her."

Michael Koons smiled. "We're more than agent and client, Isabel and me. We're symbiotic." He held up two fingers he'd intertwined. "Steady and Freddie."

"To harm her. Approach her to harm her."

The tiny man focused. "Huh? Harm her?"

He nodded. "If you have to, make up a story. Tell her you heard from someone named Mary Louise Szarsynski." He described her, including the bruises on her face. "Tell her to be alert."

Koons glared warily at the visitor. His daughter insisted he couldn't be trusted. "She's going to try to hurt her?"

"Call the police if she sees her coming."

"You're for real?"

"Tell the cops they're looking for Szarsynski for a murder in Wisconsin."

"Holy Jesus."

"As a witness."

Koons clutched his chest. "Fuck."

He didn't want to say it, but did. "Maybe she needs to go back to the ranch, Michael."

"You told your father?" Koons asked, his eyes wide in disbelief. Last Christmas, Koons drove Isabel north to the ranch and her grizzled grandfather greeted them with a pump-action .22 rifle, his eye on the sight, thinking his son was behind the wheel. It's for wolves and coyotes, he explained when he put it down. Or if he comes around, he added without smiling.

"I'll do what I can," Koons said now. "But you can't stay here. It's not going to do anybody any good."

He didn't want to leave the restaurant — questions and explanations were queued in his head — but he did, holding the glass door until a waitress passed. That's how it was now. Nobody cared what he wanted. Nobody cared what he thought. Even he no longer believed there was a way to explain. He was alive, his wife was dead, and Pup told the trades she was an orphan.

Koons returned to the table, his white trout in brown butter waiting in the shade.

"Who is that?" a colleague asked. She was Koons' age, on the dark side of 30. If she didn't make it rain soon, she'd be selling real estate in the Valley, her face on bus-stop benches.

"Isabel Jellico's father," he replied, his fork poised at his lips.

She rose out of her seat to watch him into sunlight. "He's the hobo?"

Koons chewed, swallowed, said, "Hobo in the sense that he has no fixed address. You heard they walked away from the federal witness protection program?"

She sat again. "Damned fine-looking hobo," she said.

Cherry was in a mood. Good or bad, he couldn't decide. On the upside, he'd shorted 400,000 shares of Amalgamated United and it paid off as indictments rained like confetti. Perp walks would ensue.

Meanwhile, he talked to Captain Redd, who'd flown the Alvarado brothers home. Redd described Fernando thus: "a noodle." As for Carlos, "He's got something on his mind, no?"

Cherry dialed. A woman answered. Unlike Carlos, she had an accent.

"Fernando," Cherry said.

"My brother cannot come to the phone right now."

Ah. A sister. Cherry wondered if she'd killed anybody.

"Carlos, then."

"He will call you back," she advised.

Cherry's office phone rang three minutes later.

"I hear your brother isn't doing too good."

Carlos Alvarado said, "My brother is—"

"Yeah, I know. A man. But maybe less than one hundred percent."

"He—"

"Notice how delicate I put it. Notice I didn't say he was a stuttering sack of sauerkraut."

Alvarado was at his storefront office on San Pedro, his sleeves rolled up past his elbows. Paperwork had piled up; bills begged to be paid. Without Fernando to collect, delinquencies reigned. Throughout LA County, mothers and mistresses had fingers that belonged to him in lieu of their weekly payment.

"What do you want, Cherry? Don't you have a home to go to?"

Cherry looked out his window onto Wall and Broad. At 9 o'clock at night, empty. On the building across the way, an NYPD sniper. "What's your plan, Carlos?"

"What happened to 'I don't need details'? What happened to 'Tell it to Goldsworthy'?"

"Big-picture me."

"We're going to squeeze his head until his ears meet."

Cherry laughed. "The girl. The envelope…"

"Dominoes."

"Who's tipping them? Your sister?"

"Fernando is."

"Hoo boy. Look, far be it from me to tell you your business—"

"Cherry, do you see ghosts? Because I think you do. I think you see ghosts. Cherry," Alvarado snapped. "Turn around, Cherry. Look! A ghost."

"Call Jimmy Gee."

Alvarado stopped. He said, "How do you know Jimmy Gee?"

"Insert clever phrase here, Carlos. Something snappy and hard-boiled."

Alvarado groaned out of his chair and stared at the ribbons fluttering on the air conditioner over the front door. The windows, painted yellow and red with slogans worthy of a used-car dealership, were 4 inches thick and bulletproof, the kind they use in the Popemobile. He had them installed in case he miffed Jimmy Gee, the Alvarado brothers' primo competition. Not that he was afraid of Gee, but caution rarely proved a bad investment in East LA.

He pondered. Fernando needed rest, true. Jimmy Gee could look for this Szarsynski while he concentrated on her muscle.

"I hear you thinking, Carlito…"

"You cover the cost," Alvarado replied.

"Sure," Cherry said. "What's money?"

He tried to work it through and couldn't. Every time he thought he knew the plan, it snaked where it shouldn't. He needed to be direct, to do one task at a time. Ramifications and consequences were dangerous. They could become hopeful things.

He was tired. He couldn't sleep at night. He needed distractions. Without them, the walls and ceiling were silver screens, his mind a projector.

A bar off Rampart. A dive. The tattooed waitress opened the beer bottle with her teeth.

Koons had brought him to within a single degree of Pup. For a fleeting second, less than that, he thought maybe she'd agree to his help.

After all he'd been through, he could still be naive.

Screaming, her face red and pulsing with rage, she'd said, "If for a minute you had stopped thinking about yourself, if you stopped for a second, Mom would be alive and we'd be all right.

But not you. No. No. And now look: there's nothing. You have nothing. You lost everything."

He reached for her. "Pup. Please."

She smacked at his hands as she retreated. "Look at you."

"I know, Pup."

"And now you want to drag me down. Again."

Szarsynski the liar was at hand. Szarsynski the thief.

He'd allowed himself to be drawn in. Manipulated. All this time, all those cities, and he hadn't learned a thing.

He dug into his pocket and added a dollar to the bills on the bar and drove back to the hotel. The elevator took him to his floor. He showered. He stroked his chin, wiped the mirror clean and coated his fingertips with shaving cream.

Back in the car.

He was staying in a hotel in the same chain Szarsynski used in Chicago. The concierge gave him a map of the chain's properties in the county.

On Sepulveda heading north, he turned on the radio and cranked the volume until the windows shook. He would've shouted and rattled the dash, but he'd done that before and it never made him feel any better.

CHAPTER II

He started at the perimeter, beginning in Santa Monica and circling, circling, drawing tighter toward the core. The chain had nine hotels within the circle. You guys know everything, he repeated, meaning night managers. One guy told him to fuck off; over in Silverlake, the woman behind the desk picked up the phone to call her boss. Six others watched as he pulled out a fat wad of green, unaware a half roll of quarters sat at its center for parking meters and pay phones, and then they started opening drawers and thumbing through files. It took him five hours and $358 to hear that no one had paid cash for a room around the time Mary Louise Szarsynski sent $11,000 to her mother by express mail, and no one had done so since. At least not a well-groomed young woman, pretty under her bruises, limping and rolling a suitcase behind her.

It was coming up on 5 o'clock. Sunrise soon. As he approached Highland Avenue, north of Hollywood Boulevard, he was thinking about those $11,000 she pulled out of the envelope. Ten percent? Fifty? An odd sum, 11,000. He'd held the envelope in his hands in Chicago. It was thick, but not bloated. No one crammed loose bills inside. Maybe it held 22 fresh thousand-dollar bills. If so, she's burning through it.

He needed an ATM. He crossed Gower and pulled over on Vine, just north of Sunset. He walked back to the boulevard. A short row of cars and delivery vans waited at the light. He turned the corner. There was a homeless man sitting on the sidewalk yoga-style, shoeless and crusted with dirt, a German shepherd lying at his side, chin on her paws, worry on her musty old face. They smelled of iodine and defeat. The world had ground them to powder a while ago.

The homeless man slept with his palm open, his fingers coated in grime. His clothes were held together with cord.

"You all right there, buddy?"

The guy managed to look up. He had sea-green eyes.

He gave him four five-dollar bills and the quarters.

They studied each other.

"I'm a believer," the guy said.

He went to the ATM.

He decided to walk to the last hotel. He was climbing Wilcox when his phone rang.

"Where are you, Sam?"

"You had no right."

She heard the fury in his voice. "Sam, can I explain?"

"You look at her again—"

"Sam."

"Look at her again and the cops send you back to Chicago."

"Sam, let me ex— Wait. You're not in Chicago? Where are you? Are you here, Sam?"

He didn't reply.

"I made a mistake, Sam."

"One?"

"Sam, I can't sleep." Her voice quivered. "Where are you? Are you here?"

"Then there's the Alvarado brothers," he said.

"Please be here, Sam."

"They're here too."

"I'm alone, Sam. I see that now."

What did you expect?

He turned onto Hollywood Boulevard.

"Can I apologize? I need you on my side."

He was trampling stars — Cagney, Hitchcock, Grable.

"Sam?"

"They're professionals," he said. "They know how to find people."

"The Alvarado brothers? Can they find me?"

"You're on Highland, just south of Franklin."

She was silent.

Then she whispered, "Sam, this isn't funny anymore."

Up ahead, the copper-topped turrets of Grauman's Chinese Theatre.

"Let's ask Kwame Green's four kids if it was ever funny," he said.

"Kwame Green? I know a Kwame Green. In West Allis."

"Your mother didn't—"

"I haven't spoken to my mother. You told me—"

"Alvarado shot him at your brother-in-law's shop. He's dead."

"Sam. Oh God."

"He was looking for me because he's looking for you."

"Sam, God. What did I do?"

He kept walking. He turned on Highland.

Sobbing, she said, "Oh God. Oh God. Oh God."

He held the phone away from his ear.

"Sam, be on my side. Please. Sam?"

Carlos Alvarado came down to the sounds and scents of his sister whipping up breakfast. She had five kids, and all of them — the three in Pelican Bay State Prison, the other two at Stanford — looked like walking boulders, as wide as they were tall, having left her house for school each morning with 3,600 calories on their belts. Her husband had a fatal heart attack at age 32. Now she had homemade *pan dulces* in a basket, plantains frying on the stove, the makings of *huevos Carmelita* in a bowl crooked between her arm and plump bosom. Warm tortillas waited for the eggs, ham and chorizo.

"Ah, Carmy," he said as he entered the kitchen. He kissed his sister as he jammed a clip into his Glock 32, which was the most beautiful .357 he'd ever fired. "You didn't tell me the army was coming."

She smiled politely. She didn't like Carlos. He was full of shit. Fernando was her favorite: he'd set her free. Then Carlos had turned Fernando into a killer. She didn't count the killing of their mother — that was necessary and a self-defense of sorts, according to the police. But since then, who knows how many? In his heart, Fernando was kind, considerate, a sweetie. The purple velour sweat suit she was wearing? A gift from Fernando. The Stanford tuition? Fernando. Her boys in Pelican Bay: they love their Uncle Carlos and his reputation based on the long ago. They didn't see him now. They didn't know he thought he was better than all of them, his brother and sister included.

She didn't like his kitchen either. It smelled the same as it did the day Sears delivered it. The whole house was bullshit. The exterior was beautiful, a tribute to their heritage. Inside, the furniture looked like they gave it to him for losing on "The Price is Right." It had no soul.

Carlos sat and waited for her to pour his coffee. "I see Fernando is sleeping," he said. "Was he up during the night?"

She shrugged as she returned to the stove to pour the egg mixture into a second frying pan.

Carlos spoke over the hiss. "I have to give him time to recover."

Carmelita turned. "What do you mean?"

He heard an accusation in her tone. "What do I mean? He was on the mat at death's door, Carmy. This guy knocked Fernando's brain off its stem."

"He's going to be all right. You said."

"I hope. I said I hope."

"You have to wait for him."

He reached for a hot roll. "I do?"

"You have to give him a reason to—"

"Of course, Carmy. Yes. But there is a time factor." Cherry was right. Get Jimmy Gee and act now.

She returned to the stove, working two frying pans at once. She could feel her brother staring at her. Not that ridiculous red-eye death stare that made gabacholand turn to jelly. Anyone who'd seen him posing on his toes or working with cassettes to lose his accent would laugh at that stare. This stare told her he was cooking up a bullshit lie that was supposed to remind her he was in charge.

Finally, he said, "If I let this man continue, what will they think of us?"

She adjusted the flame under the sizzling plantains and stirred the eggs.

"Really, Carmy. You tell me how I can do business with this man walking the earth."

Dishing the plantains into a bowl, she said curtly, "Fernando will feel betrayed."

"You forget that this man attacked Fernando too. He's responsible for the way he is."

"Still. He will feel you have abandoned him."

"I hope so. It would mean he is capable of understanding something."

She nodded toward the tortillas and, as Carlos slid one onto his plate, retrieved the eggs. When she served him a spoonful, he gestured for more, crooking a finger without meeting her eyes.

"Tell me this," she said as she leaned against the counter. "You're going to do this by yourself?"

He topped the meal with a tidal wave of salsa. "Eventually, yes. You know I checkmate."

"Will you tell me who you are hiring to replace our brother?"

Carlos ate eagerly, but without joy. "I don't think so," he said. "I don't see the purpose."

Fuckin' Jimmy Gee, she thought.

He paid cash for his room. Then he called Mary Louise's cell and told her to bring everything and come to 506.

Moments later, a timid knock.

He opened the door and there she was. She stared at him, clothes peeking out of her suitcase here and there, her gray jacket and skirt draped over her arm.

"Sam?"

He held out a hand to take the suitcase. "Come in," he said.

"Sam, I don't… Sam."

She was barefoot in pajama bottoms and a spaghetti-strap undershirt. Her face was yellowed, but the swelling had gone down. She looked like she hadn't eaten or slept in days.

He didn't know what to say.

She'd done something, and he was sure he'd made it worse. A good man was dead. Somebody else was going to die.

Standing there, neither in the room nor out. She stared crying. She threw herself at him. "Sam," she wailed. "What did I do?" The door closed.

He held her. She was shorter than Pup.

The money was in a safe-deposit box at a Union Bank of California branch in Pasadena. She had $46,000 left, including $800 in her wallet. She'd stolen $63,000 in thousand-dollar bills.

"Francis Cherry," she replied. "He was my boss."

She sat cross-legged on the bed. He'd made coffee in the little machine that was in the bathroom, and she cradled the cup in her hands, letting the scent rise to her face.

"I didn't mean to. Really."

"I can't begin to guess what that means," he said. He was sitting in the chair over by the desk.

"I didn't know there was money in the envelope."

Ah.

"Really," she said. "He doesn't care about money. But he was always checking the safe to make sure that envelope was in there."

"Why?"

She shook her head.

"What else is in it?"

"Two smaller envelopes. Three by five or so."

And?

"I didn't open them."

"I would have."

She sighed. "I wanted to give everything back the way it was."

"Except fifteen or so thousand dollars."

"But that's why I went to see Taylor. She knows him. She could be a go-between."

To do what?

"I could, I don't know, make good somehow. Apologize. Pay him back."

"Francis Cherry."

She nodded.

They sat in silence. She stared into the cup.

He pulled back the curtain and looked at the night.

"Cherry," she said, shaking her head. "He's unbelievable. A pig."

He waited.

"Nobody matters. He'll do anything to get his way."

And?

"I had a dream, Sam. I had plans. You know? I didn't want to be tossed aside like an old tissue."

"You slept with him?" It came out before he knew he was going to say it.

She recoiled. "My God, no. He's... God, no." She shivered.

He held up his hand to apologize.

But he wasn't there yet. He was starting to tilt her way, but the story was incomplete.

"He abused me."

"He hit you?"

"No, no, it wasn't physical, but he was abusive. Every day."

"But you didn't quit."

"It's not so simple."

Why not?

"He was always saying he was going to make sure I never worked on Wall Street again. In New York City again. Or anywhere. He was going to bury me. One phone call and I was through. He could do it."

Francis Cherry.

"The next morning, he'd act like everything was fine. Like harassment was part of the job. I'll tell you, Sam, there were times I fell for it — you know, I'd go along thinking everything was going to be all right and maybe that's the price you pay if you want to go places. Or I'd think maybe it was me. Maybe I wasn't clever enough or something."

"Clever enough for what?"

"To keep up. I'd be sitting outside his office and all these people from Wall Street, major corporations and different countries would come to see him. He'd have me bring coffee or whatever and they'd be talking and I didn't understand what they were doing in there."

"Maybe he didn't want you to know."

"The rest of the staff knew. Cherry would say a few words or make a gesture and they would jump. He'd say something to me and if I didn't get it right away, you know, what he was talking about, it would happen again. Screaming, swearing, slamming the desk. It was horrible. Humiliating."

She slid the cup on the nightstand.

"And so I did it. I took the envelope. I don't know why."

"What was your plan?"

"Plan? Sam, it was a total impulse."

All right.

"It started falling apart for me when Taylor left New York. She was a mentor, you know? She taught me everything — I couldn't find uptown from downtown before I started working for her. She was patient. She made me feel like, you know, I could belong, that I could go for what I wanted. I could seize opportunities."

Seize opportunities. Bloodless corporate-speak.

Taylor McHugh.

"She would've taken me to Chicago with her, you know? But I had to prove something to myself in New York. That's why I went there: to prove something to myself."

Chicago is a little too close to West Allis.

"So she recommended me to Cherry."

He was going to ask if McHugh knew Cherry was an abusive terror to his staff. But of course she did.

"You know," Mary Louise said, "on the plane, in the car, sitting here all alone in this hotel, I was trying to think of why. Why did I do it, Sam? Why? Why did I rip off Francis Cherry, of all people? Maybe, I don't know, maybe I had this ridiculous idea that I could have some power over him. If I took this thing, this stupid envelope that was so precious, then it would all turn around. I could stay in New York and make something out of myself. You know? Get away from his kind of corruption and live my dream. Does that make sense?"

No.

But now he understood.

No master plan. Something snaps under the weight of it all. React. Will there be consequences? No one thinks of such things when the moment arrives. Later, when what's done is done. Only then.

They sat in silence for a little while. The sun was up, traffic rushed along down on Hollywood Boulevard and across Highland, piecemealing to the 101. He liked this time of day. Its arrival meant he made it through another night.

"Is your name Sam Jellico?" she asked.

"Sam will do." It was the name the U.S. marshals had given him. Sam and Isabel Jellico, widower and daughter, moving west. Big country. Think property values, fresh air, a good school for Isabel, new friends, a new start…

"You made a mistake when you said Nathaniel Hill."

I did.

"I'm sorry I wasn't straight with you. But I was afraid you wouldn't come."

"Did you talk to my daughter?"

"I didn't. I swear."

All right.

"Please. I swear."

Yes. All right.

"Are we friends, Sam?"

He said, "I'll stand with you."

"Do you still want me to go to the police?" She was off the bed now and walking toward him.

No.

She came to him and stood inches away. Her breasts were close to his face and he could feel her heat. He looked up. Without her makeup, she had a natural beauty, a freshness fret and fear couldn't diminish.

She put her hands on his shoulders.

"Mary—"

She kissed his forehead.

"Thank you, Sam."

CHAPTER 12

Buzzed in, Jimmy Gee entered Alvarado Brothers Bail Bonds calm and slow, dripping grace, floating along the runner, and not one person in the waiting room, some of whom had been there for hours, wriggling babies on their laps, wrinkly in-laws at their sides, said word one. The man had an aura. Nobody with an aura waits.

Gee was tall and lithe, Hawaiian by birth, and he had Nefertiti eyes and hair that parted in the center to an exquisite cascade. He always wore black — 89 degrees today and he was in black: a skintight T-shirt, suede jacket, silk slacks, loafers.

What Alvarado admired most about his rival was his ability to disguise and broadcast his malevolence at the same time. His elegance didn't quite conceal his simmering viciousness nor did his lack of conscience completely deny his polish. To Alvarado, it added up to Gee being a little bit more than just another interesting shitheel on the street. He would've liked to ask him how he managed to be two things at once. But not today.

He pointed to a chair in front of his desk. "What I said on the phone. You OK with it?"

During the call, he'd told him maybe 22 percent of what happened in Chicago — after he'd probed to find out if Gee burned down Szarsynski's home.

"A job. Not a merger," Gee repeated. "After this, we go back to chasing the same scumbies."

"And you got the time?"

Gee nodded. "My time is my own."

He was a one-man operation who freelanced for points and worked out of his home. His lack of overhead contributed to an enviable profit margin.

"Where's the paper?" He crossed his leg, revealing a bare ankle.

"It's not that," Alvarado replied.

"No felony warrant?"

"Let's not focus on the guy."

"He put down your brother."

"From behind."

Gee said, "Goes without saying…"

"But he's not the mark. The girl who hired him—"

"Szarsynski," Gee said.

"You bring her to me."

He gave him the name of Taylor McHugh's hotel.

Gee made a mental note.

"Triple per-diem work for you?"

"That's fine."

"You got to spend, spend. Skim too. What the fuck. Client's got pockets down to his feet."

Alvarado let out a little laugh. He shook his head like he was relieved. "It's like this, right? Some sidebar shit and it blows up."

"I wouldn't know," Gee said as he stood.

They started out on Hollywood Boulevard. He took her to Risko, who gave her a California driver's license and a Discover card in the name of Cole K. Bennett. For $600, he threw in a Loyola Marymount student ID and a Facebook account.

"Do I look like a Cole K. Bennett?" she asked nervously as they returned to sunlight.

Everybody looks like a Cole K. Bennett, he thought. Risko had given him his first street paper, a birth certificate, hours after he realized he no longer existed.

They walked west toward Vine. She still limped a bit. He could see the Ace bandage he'd wrapped around her ankle after she dressed, sliding into green flats, jeans and a short-sleeved white cotton blouse she ironed while he cleaned up.

They wriggled through a group taking photos of the Pantages Theatre, long-dead stars beneath their feet. One man munched on a turkey leg.

She looked up at him, shielding her eyes with her hand. The sun reflected off the windshields of cars crawling past construction.

"What?" she said.

He was thinking he'd left his blazer at the hotel.

He said, "Can you listen?"

She nodded without enthusiasm. He noticed that she'd gotten smaller. Whatever spunk and spirit that survived the beating in the parking garage was just about gone.

"Cut your hair," he said.

Now it was bungeed in back. Without thinking, she gave her ponytail a gentle tug.

"Get some makeup that will cover those bruises."

He dug in his pocket and came up with his car keys.

"Then drive this to LAX and leave it at curbside."

"I've got a car—"

"I'm moving it. You want it towed. You want a DMV report."

She tried to process. The haircut and makeup she understood.

"At LAX, buy a ticket to somewhere that connects through San Diego. Be Mary Louise Szarsynski for the last time."

He'd already tossed her phone. She had another prepaid now.

"I'll meet you at the airport in San Diego. In the food court."

"Sam, I'm not… Is this going to work?"

He pointed north toward the FedEx store where she'd sent the money to West Allis.

She nodded. "Better than standing here."

He told her where he'd left his rental car.

"Can't you come with me?"

"I've got to do something first."

"Sam, I'm not sure about this."

He didn't know what to say. Nothing was easier than disappearing when no one cared where you were.

"Go, Cole."

He went toward the same ATM where he'd been a few hours ago, looking both ways as he trotted across the street.

Carmelita Alvarado had an unwavering belief in the power of a home-cooked meal. It meant love and family, and was there a better feeling than a full belly, warmth coursing through your veins, every sense sated? No. There was not.

Fernando was sprawled on his back, unperturbed by the sunlight pouring into the guest room. He had an erection, causing his boxers to tent. She took that as a sign of recovery.

"Fernando," she whispered, trying to avoid the gruesome bruise on his beautiful face. "Fernando."

He opened his eyes slowly and fluttered his long eyelashes. She pictured a prizefighter who wasn't sure he could rise from the canvas.

"Hey, lazy bird," she said in Spanish. "It's lunchtime."

He lifted his head from the pillow and smacked his lips, removing cobwebs. "Carmy?" he said, confused.

"Fernando..." she purred.

He groped to find the top sheet and tugged it to cover his bottom half. "Where's Carlos?"

That bastard. "He went to the office. Fernando, how do you feel?"

He frowned.

"Better?" She clasped his hand.

"Carmy..." he said helplessly.

"You can get out of bed?"

He looked at her.

OK, he's not exactly blank, she thought, but he doesn't have the full picture.

Then he turned on his side. When he brought up his knees, she saw a baby in the womb.

"Listen, lazy bird, I didn't come here to watch you sleep all day."

The anti-seizure medicine was bullshit. They were doping him so bad, no wonder he stumbled like a half-wit. All he needed was Tylenol, sun and a few good meals prepared with loving care.

"Come on." She lifted the sheet at the foot of the bed and tickled his insole. It was probably a good thing that he curled his toes.

"Carmy. Did you cook, Carmy?" The words came slow, but they had a little bit of inflection.

"*Sopa de higaditos,*" she said. Chicken livers in a thick broth. "That'll get you going like Valvoline."

"You bring it to me, Carmy."

"Fuck no," she told him. "We get you a shower and then you come downstairs with me."

She pinched his Achilles tendon, and he kicked out his leg.

"Hop to it, lazy bird," she said as she stood.

Jimmy Gee slid a gift certificate for $10,000 to Jimmy Choo's in a thank-you card, sealed the envelope and gave it to the clerk at McHugh's boutique hotel, slipping a 50 along with it into her little brown hand. Call her down, he said. She dialed and he put his finger across his lips. Then he picked up his briefcase, went back outside and talked the merits of his BMW X5 to the valet, its black body shining in the midday sun. Then he told him not to touch it.

McHugh came to the desk in a big straw hat and iris-blue sarong, a sheer thing that revealed a bikini underneath. She accepted the envelope, opened it and removed her sunglasses to examine its contents.

Hmm, thought Jimmy Gee, as he peered into the lobby. She's not surprised. Lady knows somebody who'd drop a nice slice of cash in gratitude.

He was at the rooftop pool before she returned. Under a cabana's shelter, he opened his briefcase. For cover, he ordered lunch — grilled shrimp with a mango dressing and a split of a melony Santa Barbara pinot grigio. McHugh reclaimed her station poolside, her long legs by now a golden brown, freckles appearing above her breasts. Gee saw a glimmer of pride in her bearing, a thin smile of satisfaction. But she didn't give much and he couldn't make it back to its source — whether she was glad for the approval of whoever she thought sent the gift certificate or whether she thought she'd played the mark right.

He hid in plain sight, aware that every woman at the pool was trying to catch his eye. Half the men too. He put up a shield by making like he was diving heavy into business e-mail on his PDA, a tricked-out model a mark crafted for him. By the time the meal arrived, he had off-loaded the contents of McHugh's cell. By the time he topped off the chilled glass of white, he figured by McHugh's call pattern he had Szarsynski's cell or one that belonged to the guy Alvarado wanted teed-up, the guy he called a ranch-hand bum.

If he took down the man Alvarado wanted, he thought as he stood and wafted toward the elevator, it would get back to the contractor that Jimmy Gee was the shit in LA.

Gee located the cell's signal. Highland, off Hollywood Boulevard. Maybe a 10-minute drive.

He parked at the hotel's loading dock near a Dumpster overflowing with soggy cardboard and the odor of rancid fish, and entered the air-conditioned lobby. Until he stepped into the elevator, he kept the pulsing handheld hidden — in the elevator too, given the security camera — and got off on the third floor.

No.

Fourth, via the stairs.

No.

He walked up to the fifth. The tracking signal was stronger now.

Two maids' carts clogged the corridor. The women were behind doors held ajar by the security bar. They watched soaps on TV while they worked, and they kept the volume loud enough so they could hear while vacuums whirred and water ran.

He kept going. No one saw him.

He stopped outside room 506.

A DO NOT DISTURB sign was hung on the knob. A room service tray sat sentrylike on the carpet. Gee looked down. Food for two. Famished or stocking up for a trip. One of them had licked the plates.

Gee dipped long fingers into a jacket pocket and removed a forklike device that would undo the security bar. He slipped it between his teeth as he reached to his ankle for his Taurus Mil Pro. Then he produced a universal keycard.

Squared, silent amid the ricocheting noise in the hallway, Gee went to work with poise and speed: the lock opened, the security bar popped back and he slid in sideways, as graceful as a dancer. His pistol was raised to eye level, his arm just so.

On the floor, staring at his reflection in the TV, was a wild-haired man covered in soot and grime, his clothes held together with cord. But a crisp blue blazer draped his shoulders like a cape.

On the bed, a mottled German shepherd.

On the credenza, a cell phone.

"I'm a believer," the homeless man said, tugging a lapel.

Recoiling from the foul scent, Gee glanced at the dog up on the soft king. The dog smiled.

Swiping the phone, jabbing it in his side pocket, Gee calculated, nipping at the inside of his cheek. The homeless man saw him.

Szarsynski gives up her muscle to Alvarado, the guy winds up dead and found, and the homeless guy says, "Oh, Jimmy Gee."

TVs and vacuum cleaners down along the hallway blared.

Gee flexed his finger near the trigger.

Suddenly, the dog snarled. She bared her rotted teeth.

"I'm a believer," the guy repeated. He had a bottle of A.1. sauce in his hand, holding it like a cold beer.

Next door, the vacuuming stopped.

The dog stood, ready to pounce.

Gee spun and hit her between the eyes with the gun butt.

The old dog yelped, then plopped on her side.

Alarmed, the homeless man struggled to stand. But Gee kicked him in the chest. When the man fell back, Gee stood over him. Grimacing, he put his arm over his nose to block the stench.

Gee pointed the gun at his face.

The man had sea-green eyes.

"Excuse me," sang a cleaning lady as she rapped on the door. "Housekeeping."

Fuck. The cleaning lady, the skank, the dog and then whoever else heard the shots…

"Call security," Gee shouted.

The woman peeked in.

"Security," Gee insisted, showing her the gun.

On the bed, the dog began to stir.

Gee raised his foot to drive his heel into the homeless man's face. But the man, who knew how to take a hit like he'd been beaten before, quickly rolled into a helpless ball.

Gee backed out. He strode toward the fire stairs.

It didn't matter that he'd given up his phone. Pup wasn't going to call. Especially if Koons told her he was nearby. Now he really was among the invisible, the link severed. No longer drifting, he was gone.

In San Diego, Cole K. Bennett was waiting in the air-conditioned food court.

He eased into a chair at the table next to hers, away from airport bustle.

She was startled, then relieved. Then she said, "I didn't think you were coming." The Surfliner out of LA's Union Station took nearly three hours to reach his destination. "Sam, listen, I've been having second thoughts. Maybe you were right. Maybe I should just go to the police."

"Alvarado will know where you are," he replied. "The cops can't protect you forever. Not even for long."

"What if I gave it back? I mean, I could fly to New York and give it back."

She'd been crying. The short haircut made her seem younger and fragile.

"You see Frances Cherry as a man who will let it go?" he asked.

"I never opened the little envelopes."

"Maybe he can hold off the Alvarados. Maybe. He stood, towering over her. He said, "Maybe there's a way to work this out."

"I don't see it, Sam. I'm trying, but I can't find a solution."

"We're not the only ones in this."

"Not the—" She paused. "My mom."

"Your mom."

"Your daughter, maybe."

"Not unless you tipped off McHugh."

"I didn't. I swear."

"All right…"

"I do swear, Sam." Then she said, "You didn't use the name Nathaniel Hill with anybody else, did you?"

I still didn't know why I did that.

He said, "And maybe we owe Kwame Green's family."

"Not maybe. No, we do."

"So we have to see this through." He held out his hand.

She accepted his gesture and lifted out of her seat.

Years of business travel had resulted in countless meals alone for Taylor McHugh. Room service was always substandard, even at five-star hotels, and vaguely pathetic, especially at five-star hotels. So she'd take herself to dinner, as she did tonight, on a recommendation from the concierge, who called ahead to secure a table for one. The restaurant, on La Cienega, was austere, minimalist even, which suited her. The table for one gave an illusion of privacy and the wait staff was attentive. She ordered the six-course tasting menu with the wine pairing. An extravagance, though after this afternoon's windfall, not really. The seared foie gras was excellent, as was the braised veal cheek. The wine went to her head.

"Francis?"

She'd never call if she wasn't approaching giddy.

"It's two in the morning," Cherry said.

"No, it's only eleven. Where are you?"

For some reason, he'd been hankering for German food and wound up in a biergarten on the Lower East Side. Hoisting barrel-size steins, a group of businessmen from Cologne kept eyeing him, and for the hell of it, he went over and joined them. Now they were elbowing a poker table in a new marble-and-glass penthouse overlooking downtown Manhattan. The Germans had so many tells they might as well play with their cards facing out. He was up $14,000 and knew which *telekom* the Bundesrat was taking public. The Germans liked him. The way he gutted a vice president of the U.S. subsidiary was ruthlessly efficient. Clearly, Mr. Cherry's parents had managed to flee the fatherland after the war.

"Why are you calling?"

The Germans tried to listen in.

McHugh said, "I want to thank you for your gratuity."

She was in the narrow vestibule by the rest room. Lifting her cell from her handbag had resulted in three waiters rushing her table to declare the restaurant's no-phone policy.

"You're welcome. What gratuity?"

Oh shit. Stumbling, she said, "Did I say gratuity? I meant graciousness. Giving me extra time and all…"

"Put it to good use." He had a pair of threes and would play them like he had five aces.

"Well then, Francis—"

He held up a finger, asking the Germans for a moment. They suspected subterfuge.

He stood. "This gratuity…"

"No, I meant—"

"Did it come with an attachment?"

She couldn't very well acknowledge the thank you card. "I don't get you."

"Like a Mexican guy. Hard. Some kind of evil eyes." Cherry hadn't seen a photo of Carlos Alvarado. Goldsworthy couldn't come up with one.

"No…"

"What was it? The gratuity."

"A gift certificate to Jimmy Choo's. Ten thousand dollars."

"Hoo boy. That's a lot of shoes."

She raised a hand to her forehead. "Francis, maybe it's better if I call you in the morning."

"No, no," he said. "I'm intrigued. I'll call you."

"Francis, let me clarify—"

He went back to the poker table. He sat, bloated with the sense of well-being that came with taking down *dummköpfe* who think they can't be beat.

She freshened up, studying for a moment the highlights in her hair. As she returned to the vestibule, she was greeted by a man she'd seen somewhere. Recently too. The wine, damn it. How else could she forget a man like this?

"It's always business," he said with a smile.

"Does it show?"

"Actually, no. To be honest, I was admiring how much you enjoyed your dinner."

Cherry and the flubbed phone call made the meal seem like it happened days ago.

"*Savored* your dinner," he amended.

"It was… Well, it was fabulous," she replied.

The man with the Nefertiti eyes said, "Would it be inappropriate for me to ask you to join me for a nightcap?"

"Oh, I don't—"

He brushed his fingers on her arm. "I'll confess. I saw you at the pool today. When I came in and saw you here, I thought…" He seemed to blush. "I shouldn't tell you what I thought."

That hair. She would kill to have silky hair with that kind of shine. And there was something else. An air of quiet self-confidence. An aura.

He was lean. And golden. And beautiful.

"At your table?" the man in black prodded. "My tab. Your table."

He swept his arm toward the opening to the dining room.

CHAPTER 13

Gee ran his hand over her bare bottom. She moaned a little bit, turned and smiled his way. He was already showered and dressed, a haloed vision in black, backlit by thin streams of morning sun.

"Honey…" she managed. What a deep and peaceful sleep.

"A full day for me," he replied.

She turned and upped on her elbows, as naked as a newborn. "Breakfast, though…"

He looked at his watch. He was done here, but what the hell. "Pick me up at the business center."

"Mmmm," Taylor McHugh said, nodding.

Driving east on Pico, Carlos Alvarado tried to remember the old days. Once he'd threatened to a tie a rival's baby son to a Dunlop on his low-rider and drive East LA *bajito y suavecito*, and he would've done it, no problem and no remorse. (Instead, he bit off the tip of the man's nose.) Back then, he didn't give a fuck. He walked like a man. The street revered his name. But in Chino, he saw the future. Every baldy in the joint was broken. Grooming his nephews wasn't going to give him back lost time. Immortality wasn't happening.

The only people who seemed anywhere near content wore suits and slung a briefcase.

And so…

He'd turned himself inside out and it worked.

Until someone took down Fernando, and in turn Carlos killed a bystander. He couldn't track down the man he wanted. He was exposed. He *needed*.

If you told him two weeks ago he would call in Jimmy Gee, he would've laughed in your face. And then sent Fernando to blow-torch your eyebrows.

He had to get his edge back.

Like it was in hiding, waiting for his call.

Like it still existed somewhere else.

Traffic up ahead so he turned north on Roxbury, going back to move ahead on Olympic.

In addition to everything else, his sister Carmelita, whose presence unnerved him. The sound of her slippers slapping the kitchen floor sent him back decades — his mother devil-screeching and taking a sawed-off broomstick to the back of his head, his father toweling off the blood, whispering "I love you, Carlito. Please. No to worry. God is watching." Carmy was Mama and Papi rolled into one, the queen of kick-and-kiss. As he entered his own kitchen he saw she wouldn't mind if he dropped dead twice. And yet on the table was a feast prepared with love. She was making him crazy.

"I'm taking Fernando out today." She was especially defiant this morning, though she wore a velour tracksuit that made her look like a ripe orange.

"You took him out yesterday," Carlos replied. He sat before a tower of her cornmeal cakes spiked with jalapeños.

"Are you spying on me?"

"He fell down at Ralphs, Carmy, in the kosher-food aisle. You don't think I'd know?"

"He needs exercise."

"And matzos?"

He turned onto La Cienega. Last night, unable to sleep with his siblings under his roof — maybe their parents would crawl out of hell, wormed and muddy to join them — he concluded he wasn't going to normalize until that ranch-hand bum was toe-tagged. Let's keep it simple, he decided. Be prompt. Let Jimmy Gee do what he's doing and I'll do what I've got to do and we'll put this nightmare behind us. Carmy goes home and maybe Fernando can relearn the alphabet and how to tie his shoes and stick a .686 into a runner's ear, get our money and then blow his brains out the other side while I make business.

So satisfying was the thought of life at Alvarado Brothers Bail Bonds returning to standard that he lingered in his reverie and didn't notice the traffic light had changed. Now, with the morning sun high over Restaurant Row, he was assaulted by an ugly chorus of blaring car horns.

They'd had a productive day in San Diego. He bought six shirts, a blazer and a prepaid cell phone. Cole K. Bennett felt guilty about spending while Kwame Green's kids were without a father. But he insisted. He dragged her into stores, waiting patiently, avoiding memories of shopping with Pup by pretending he was Jimmy Stewart remaking Kim Novak in "Vertigo." Reminded himself that sentiment is an enemy. Then he saw a suit his wife would've worn. Suddenly, Moira was right there. She smiled. She called him by his true name. He was going to ask if she'd forgiven him. But she was gone.

They bought a car up near Palmdale, a '98 Escort that shimmed up I-5 even when Cole drove the slow lane. No one who saw her puttering by would guess she was sitting on $46K.

In Pasadena, he rented a furnished two-bedroom, not far from the bank where she'd hid Cherry's envelopes.

Cole insisted they buy new pillows and sheets. He'd never done that. He always slept on the sofa.

He read while she washed the new bedding in a Laundromat in Van Nuys, the machines thumping and whirling, soap scent filling the air.

"How does it end, Sam?"

Took him a minute to realize she meant the book. "Justice prevails," he replied. "It's fiction."

They had In-and-Out burgers.

She woke up around midnight and found him sitting in the living room, fully dressed and staring at his hands.

She wore the strawberry pajamas he'd picked up at JC Penney.

"Can't sleep?" she asked.

Won't.

"Want company?"

No. No company.

"Tell me if you want to," she said, leaning against the door frame. "If you want to talk."

That man killed my wife. The thug's son, the machine. Everything else is periphery.

She was still sleeping when he left to drive down to Orange County. He wanted a Smith & Wesson 910 worth $650 out of the box.

Gee had every kind of tool he needed to find anyone anywhere in North America, but he preferred setting a baseline by working the Web. The Web was linear. Instincts and creativity were required; an ox like Alvarado had neither. In the right mind, one piece of information flowed to another and there you were.

The area code on a phone number in McHugh's cell led him to several stories in Wisconsin newspapers about a murder in West Allis.

At Melenchuk's Heating, Ventilating and Air Conditioning.

And how some guy named Roger Melenchuk married a woman named Bonnie Szarsynski seven years ago in West Allis.

And how Mary Louise Szarsynski was godmother to Jim Morrison Melenchuk, son of Roger and Bonnie.

He discovered all of this in the hotel's business center while McHugh readied, using a computer available to anyone passing through the lobby to the parking garage.

In maybe five minutes, while the guy at the other computer checked the ball scores, he learned Carlos Alvarado shot and killed Kwame Green. The wrong man.

She came down sparkling. Reserved. Contained. But sparkling in sandals, pearl slacks and a gold top, arriving in reception as Gee read The Wall Street Journal.

He stood, unfolding with ease.

"Good morning," she said, thrusting out her hand.

Gee shook it and remembered how she rode him sweat-soaked on the balcony, her hips swaying as he nipped at her surprisingly perfect breasts.

"There's a little place around the corner. Organic coffees, whole-grain breads…"

She waited as Gee returned the newspaper to the front desk.

When they stepped outside, she hooked her arm in his, the charade at reception abandoned.

"Jimmy, I had a time last night," Taylor McHugh said. "I have to tell you, I had a time."

They walked in lockstep.

"But it's good-bye," she added. "You know that."

"I do," Jimmy Gee replied.

"No regrets?"

"How could there be?"

She liked that. That was good. "When I'm alone in my apartment on a frigid night in New York City…"

Chicago, Gee thought. Overlooking the lake, and the Ferris wheel on the Navy Pier.

"I'll remember you."

Fascinating, thought Gee. No blink, no twitch, no tell. This *haole* bitch would short-circuit a lie detector. She's a soul made of steel.

Carlos Alvarado stared into the rearview and watched Jimmy Gee stroll off with a blonde who had to be Taylor McHugh, Cherry's mole.

Holy shit.

Look at him, petting her hand. Cooing.

Scheming to work me over.

He punched the steering wheel, sending a shock to his ribs.

A setup.

A motherfucking setup.

Cherry.

He's turned it over to Jimmy Gee.

Why?

What says to Cherry that Jimmy Gee's a better man than me?

Double-trouble New York fuck Cherry.

I ought to take Cherry's balls and—

Alvarado stopped. He held up his hand. He took a deep breath.

"*Tranquilo*," he said. "*Tranquilo.*"

He counted to 10 before picking up his cell.

In New York, Cherry looked up to find his new secretary in his office.

"A Mr. Alvarado for you," she said with a faux breezy flair he'd soon find annoying.

"Give it to Goldsworthy."

She blinked in confusion. Goldsworthy?

"Never mind," he said as he pawed for the phone. He waited until she disappeared.

"Carlos, give me your definition of discretion. Help me understand."

"I know what you're up to, Cherry."

"Do tell."

"But Jimmy Gee is playing you. Jimmy Gee is smarter than you."

"Ergo, since you believe yourself smarter than Jimmy Gee…"

"He is fucking your Taylor McHugh."

Cherry frowned. "Literally? Figuratively?"

"For real."

"That doesn't answer—"

"I saw them. She hears wedding bells. Maybe you will be the best man."

Cherry paused as he tried to imagine McHugh with her clothes off, her body bare and unadorned. Sliding his palm across his clean-shaven head, he said, "Tell me about this Gee."

"No, Cherry, you tell me." Alvarado's voice lapsed into singsong. "Cherry, I think there are newsmen and TV cameras in the lobby. Oh, wait, now everyone is moving toward the elevators. Go open your office door, Cherry. Let those bright lights shine on you."

"Talk to Gee," Cherry said, "and I'll get in touch with McHugh."

"Or maybe they got handcuffs," Alvarado repeated. "Me, I think you last eleven minutes in prison. No, eight. Three."

Cherry stroked his chin.

"Cherry?"

Goldsworthy. Jesus. He insisted Carlos Alvarado was going to retrieve his envelopes, take his payment and go. There was no percentage in doing anything else. Goldsworthy said Alvarado was happy running his lucrative bail bonds business, so much so that he was looking to expand. Cherry told Goldsworthy to intimate the possibility of entry into the New York market.

But who knew anything about this Gee? Goldsworthy said he was almost as good as Fernando Alvarado in bringing them back tuned up and contrite. The standard: Fernando, who ended up in a coma.

But if Gee made an alliance with McHugh…

Carlos Alvarado said, "Hey Cherry, here come the handcuffs."

Cole K. Bennett woke up to find him gone. No note, no explanation. His new blazer hung in the closet in the other bedroom, but the bed hadn't been touched. On the empty chest of drawers was the receipt from the Chinese laundry for his shirts, and two paperback books he'd bought. That little kit bag he picked up was open, the toiletries used and tucked back inside. He'd shaved, showered. The towel was still damp.

She strolled barefoot toward the living room where she caught a little bit of his scent. She tried to imagine him sitting there, tall, lean, a mop of sandy hair, that teardrop scar at the side of his eye, the vacant expression on his face. Every now and then he frowned. He grimaced, as if a painful memory had suddenly appeared. Then he'd shake his head and soon the vacant look would return.

She went to the window to peer past the fire escape and down into the alley. The car they bought was gone.

She let the curtain flutter.

Alone, she felt a rush of insecurity. Suddenly, the world seemed very large and she seemed very small.

She hurried to her phone.

Noon greeted Jimmy Gee at Zuma, where he sat watching the crowd on the beach, the swimmers in the surf, a helicopter as it hovered over a distant pad. The sun nestled on his black shirt and baked his skin. He slipped off his calfskin loafers.

He was running through what he'd learned since he left Alvarado's office. The guy who was advising Szarsynski had hid her good, closing down her cell and charge cards. Her car had been towed from a hydrant at Sunset and Las Palmas, and that was smart. Szarsynski bought a ticket to Juarez via San Diego, but Gee knew she wasn't going into Mexico. The guy wasn't going to let her use her passport. Maybe she stayed in San Diego. Maybe she was a thousand miles away. Maybe that was Szarsynski in the red tankini tiptoeing into the surf.

The only mistake the guy made was Risko, who gave them up without a fight, without Gee's Taurus coming off his ankle.

Cole K. Bennett, a student at Loyola Marymount. For her driver's license, an address in Marina del Rey that Risko pulled off Yahoo! Maps.

"You came sooner, Jimmy, and I would've coded the license," Risko said, holding up his hands in surrender.

Risko took a smack for that.

Szarsynski's guy bought a new name a couple of years ago. Leslie Hope of Carson City, Michigan. No, Lester. Lester Hope.

"His real name," Gee said.

"He never told me," Risko replied, quaking.

Soon his lip bled.

Gee took half the money Szarsynski gave Risko.

Gee didn't think much of going back to Alvarado and telling him he'd found a void.

He was thinking in the long run maybe he didn't have to go back to Alvarado at all.

McHugh had been calling New York in clusters — bars, restaurants, health clubs. And two cells, many times. One belonged to an Ian Goldsworthy, a U.K. resident whose occupation was listed as butler. He was employed by Cerasus Partnership LLP, which was registered in the Cayman Islands, but had a subsidiary with an office on Broad Street, Francis Cherry Investment Counseling. McHugh had called the office several times, and had received calls from a number assigned to the building. The other cell she called was registered to Cerasus too, and Gee figured it was Francis Cherry's.

With two calls from a pay phone, Gee learned that Mary Louise Szarsynski worked for Cherry Investments. She had been Francis Cherry's secretary until a few weeks ago.

Gee took a short leap of faith and figured it was Cherry or his man Goldsworthy who hired Alvarado to bring back Szarsynski. A week into her disappearance, she called McHugh on her cell in Chicago. In Chicago, where the ranch-hand bum put the Alvarado brothers in the hospital.

Szarsynski had something, or knew something, that meant enough to Cherry that he'd climbed in bed with the Alvarados.

McHugh knows what it is.

And whatever it is, it's worth more than triple per-diem on a job designed to make Gee's rival look good.

Gee picked up his shoes and walked the incline to the beach. He wanted warm sand between his toes. He wanted the breeze off the wrong side of the Pacific to blow through his hair. He was sitting in the middle of something fine — a chance to make more than a little money while putting Carlos Alvarado on the downslide.

It could be awfully sweet.

CHAPTER 14

He got a gun. Not the one he wanted, but a nine with a full clip. He knew his way around guns, and not just because his father crammed a rifle in his hand as soon as he could stand tall and walk. He'd stolen a pistol from the cash register drawer at a bar and grill up in Carlotta where he worked as a dishwasher. The man's wife was spotty and given to long rants. She would've been blamed and in time would've confessed. He returned it the next day, certain he owed the troubled couple more than hard work for taking him in. He was 15 years old.

New gun nearby, he drove the shimmying Escort to a hardware store and bought two alarms for the apartment in Pasadena, one for the front door, one for the window to the fire escape. They had pepper spray at the counter, so he bought a canister fit for a key ring. It wouldn't stop the Alvarados, but it might make Cole feel a little more secure. She'd tossed all night, muttered and moaned, and he thought maybe he'd heard her grind her teeth.

He changed out his prepaid cell for another. He left the new number on Michael Koons' voice mail at the agency.

He stopped at a garage and had them look at the car. They fixed a bent wheel and he bought four new tires. While he waited, he closed his eyes to rest. He needed sleep. His mind was foggy. He nodded off and saw Pup. Of course he did: He'd looked in while Cole K. Bennett took her troubled sleep, like he'd do in wonder when Pup was a child.

He went across the road and had a fish taco.

The sky was endless, a perfect blue, and the palm trees swayed in the sun. He pulled off the 110 to get supplies. The way Cole looked into the empty refrigerator told him, like the new bedding and towels, that she was thinking of settling in. She needed a home. He didn't.

He parked the car in the alley behind the apartment building in Pasadena.

He was thinking she could find a job in finance downtown. On Metro Rail, the Gold Line to the Red Line would put her in Bunker Hill.

He opened the trunk, hoisted two shopping bags and the sack from the hardware store and went into the building.

It had a rattling elevator, but he decided to walk the three flights.

Juggling the bags, he knocked on the door.

He said, "It's me, Cole."

Then he said, "Cole?"

He wriggled the key out of his jeans.

"Talk to me," Alvarado said from behind his desk.

"Not on a cell," Gee replied.

"Come to the office."

"There's nothing to say."

Alvarado sat forward. "Let me assure you that you do not—"

Gee opened Alvarado's door and stepped into the cluttered suite, snapping his phone shut. "Quick enough?"

Oh yeah, I'm ready for the streets, Alvarado thought as he puffed his cheeks and put down the handset. Sure I am. I've got video on the front and back doors, monitors over there on the table, Jimmy Gee walks up and I see shit. Oh yeah.

Gee sat, wiping errant grains of sand from his slacks. "Szarsynski is Cole K. Bennett now, a student at Loyola Marymount. She's not, of course, but she's in LA."

"Cherry doesn't want you fucking with his mole."

Gee didn't blink. "Cherry?"

"You want to play it like that? Fine. But you strip her cell, you know Cherry."

"Is he one of the New York numbers?"

"Everything flows through me."

Gee shrugged. "Your ranch-hand bum bought a car in San Diego. Lester Hope is the name he's using."

"You check FasTrak?"

"Nothing. He's paying tolls with coin. If he's got a credit card as Hope, he's not using it."

Gee slipped his long fingers into an inside jacket pocket and produced two passport-size photos. He slid them across the desk.

Alvarado stared at one photo. "He lost weight."

"That photo was taken at least two years ago."

"And this is Szarsynski."

"That is Cole K. Bennett, yes."

Alvarado said, "And all this from one night with Taylor McHugh."

"None of this is from Taylor McHugh. At least not directly."

"Let that go, Jimmy."

Gee stood.

"Jimmy…"

That voice. That stare. Maybe it worked on meter maids, but the ranch-hand bum caved in his ribs and Alvarado hadn't seen him coming. For a man from South Central, that's beyond weak.

"It's your play, Carlos," Gee replied. "By the way, I'm down fifteen grand."

"Money is not an issue," Alvarado told him as he opened a desk drawer. "Just stand clear of Cherry. I mean it."

The Union Bank of California had eight branches in and around Pasadena. Not every one offered safe-deposit boxes. He put on his new blazer, parked the Escort, walked in and showed the photo Risko gave him to the security guards. "Have you seen this girl?"

No.

"Why?" one guard said. She was lean, young and black and she wore her gun high like she was dying to pull it. "This girl. She your daughter?"

No sign of struggle and she'd taken some of the clothes from the apartment.

But it was looking like Cole K. Bennett left without Cherry's money and his envelopes.

He sat in the car and called local taxi companies.

No, they didn't pick up a young woman outside the address he gave.

Nearby?

The dispatchers grew impatient and so did he.

He gave a moment's thought to calling the cops.

He was standing under the sun on Colorado Boulevard. He watched the buses as they passed. One was heading for the airport in Burbank.

He called her cell again and left another message.

He said, "If you still have your old credit card, don't use it. Run if you have to, but stay Cole Bennett."

He drove to the airport. He was sweating, and he knew he looked harried. He needed a shower. Sleep too. He took a deep breath.

He talked to ticket agents. He talked to security personnel. He talked to checkers. He talked to every driver in the taxi queue.

"We had… It was a misunderstanding," he said if they asked.

No one admitted to seeing her.

"She's my daughter."

Maybe Alvarado did take her. Maybe he's so damned smooth he could make it look like she walked away.

He'd lost all sight of the woman who ripped off Francis Cherry. Who snuck out of the hospital, leaving a worried mother behind. Who lied, telling him Alvarado burned down her family home.

He saw her crying. He saw her slumped and abandoned in the food court. He saw her in those strawberry pajamas.

His phone buzzed.

"It's John Bleak," he said into the prepaid cell.

"John Bleak," said Taylor McHugh. She sat up on the lounge chair and slid her magazine next to a tube of suntan lotion, the sun high above the Hollywood hills.

"Mary Louise," he said. "Have you heard from her?"

"Why call me?"

"Because she believes you can help her. Have you?"

"No. Where are you, Mr. Bleak?"

A jet roared off the runway not 500 yards away.

McHugh said, "I'm in Los Angeles. That's a sign of good faith, by the way."

"Why…?"

"Why?"

"Why are you in Los Angeles?"

"I have a job, Mr. Bleak. On occasion, I travel."

"She trusts you."

"Well, she should. I tried to tell you that. Whatever she's in, I'll do what I can to help her get out."

He drove back to the bank branches with safe-deposit boxes. He dropped a C-note on each guard and gave them his cell number. Please, he said.

McHugh walked to the swimming pool, dipped a toe and stepped into the shallow end. She sat on a middle step, letting the cool water rush along her thighs and stomach. Five minutes later, she returned to her lounge chair.

"Tell Francis she's coming to me," she said to Goldsworthy, Cherry's security chief, shouldering her cell phone as she toweled down.

"We're certain, are we?" Goldsworthy asked, a note of hope in his voice.

"Ian…" she sighed. She'd never thought much of his colonial airs. Cherry had tried to turn a crude mercenary into a reasoned source of intelligence. He failed.

"Did you tell her where you are?" he asked.

"She knows where I stay in LA."

"Would—"

"It's a matter of when, of course. But she's coming here."

Carlos Alvarado pulled his car into the scoop in front of his house, keeping an eye on a pudgy little boy on the grassy circle. The boy was playing catch with Fernando, who wore a bandana across his forehead, a short-sleeve work shirt buttoned at the collar, drooping jeans and no shoes. When the boy tossed a spongy red ball to him, he snatched at it without grace, his face pinched in concentration. Then he made a puny underhand return throw, and the ball landed well short of its mark. Thinking that was the game, the barefoot kid was happy to retrieve it.

Carmelita was sitting on the front steps, a bag of homemade *chicharrón* at her side.

"Who's Short Pants?" Carlos said, as he put his briefcase on the walk.

"That's your grandnephew," she replied. "Dodo's boy."

"Dodo in Chino, six years into seventeen?"

"My Dodo, yes."

"And he has a three-year-old?"

"Like you never heard of conjugal," she said.

Sliding down his tie, Carlos nodded in admiration. "Another question, Carmy." He pointed toward Fernando.

She said, "He looks great, doesn't he?"

Carlos saw a saggy facsimile of his brother, a straw man, herky-jerky in slo-mo.

"I would say no. He doesn't look great."

"He looks better."

"I'll give you that." Carlos remembered his brother in his coma, sprouting tubes, machines doing the work. Last rites given.

"Fernando," Carmelita shouted, "tell Carlos how you're doing."

"Soon I will be able to go back to work," Fernando said. The evening sun gave his skin a yellowish hue, and the dent in his head cast a shadow on his nose.

"You tell him to say that?" Carlos whispered to his sister.

"Encourage him, Carlos. Be a brother."

All right. "Fernando," he shouted, "maybe you should go play for the Dodgers."

Dodo's son threw the ball. It hit Fernando in the chest and plopped to the turf.

An hour later, Carlos Alvarado entered the kitchen to a feast. Pork chops in adobe sauce, white beans, fresh corn, *bolillos* — Dodo's kid was chomping on a hot roll now, kicking his bare feet.

Fernando sat upright with his back to the wall, the bandana gone, his hands beneath the crowded table. Evening sunlight surrounded him, and Carmy's crucifix hung on the wall above his head. The kitchen smelled like heaven on a holiday.

Over by the stove, Carmelita was spooning rice into another bowl Carlos didn't know he owned.

Without turning, she shouted, "Go!"

Fernando stood, raised a nine from under the table and pointed it at his brother.

Startled, Carlos angled to reduce the target. Then he sagged. He muttered his brother's name.

Fernando struggled to stand tall. His arm trembled, the gun quivered.

Dodo's boy watched without interest.

"Carmy..." Carlos said, glancing sideways.

The bowl of steaming rice in her hands, Carmelita approached the table. "In only one day of practice, he can do this."

Fernando had his finger on the trigger.

"Enough," Carlos said to his sister. "Point made. The man got the drop on me."

But even in his flabby state, by now Carlos could've grabbed the boy as a shield and backed away. He could've disarmed his brother, jammed the nine under his chin and sent his brains through the roof. Back in the day, he would've finished dinner with blood and tissue dripping from the beams.

Fernando's eyes rolled in his head.

"You're saying you believe in him?" Carmelita asked.

"Fernando, let's eat," Carlos said, nodding toward the food. "Carmy, tell him."

She did. Fernando sat slowly and put the gun on his plate.

Cherry wondered what it was like to tail somebody. If a semi-simian like Alvarado could do it…

In the late afternoon, he saw a tour group coming out of the Stock Exchange just as he was leaving for a meeting. They gathered around a woman. She was tall with long, thick black hair, wide face and cheeks and she spoke Italian, gesturing like her fingers were on fire. Hmm, thought Cherry. He blew off the meeting and, to keep the New York sun from shining off his notable dome, stepped into the shadows on Nassau Street, peeking. The group went inside the Federal Building and Cherry climbed to the statue of George Washington, maybe he wound up in 800 photos taken by Japanese tourists, but what the fuck. When the Italian beauty walked out, he was behind her. The tour group got on the bus, "*Ciao, ciao. Arrivederci.*" Fumes, the bus took off and, counting her tip, she went down into the subway. When she got off in Little Italy, Cherry was still on her notable ass.

Now he was sitting in a café on Mott Street. She was serving cappuccinos and cannoli over there to fanny-pack tourists in search of Don Corleone. Little Italy was a joke, a cartoon. The Italy pavilion at Epcot had more soul. The defamation league should boycott. Meanwhile, leathery old men in baggy suit jackets came by and nodded at Cherry, who gave a little circular wave between sips of espresso. Fredos in red vests gathered to look at him, their expressions revealing a touch of fear, and pretty soon she approached, powdered sugar on the front of her stupid little uniform. She spoke in Italian, thinking she was addressing some out-of-town capo. Then, in English, she said, "My Uncle Vito would be honored if you would come to our shop, Signore…"

"Ciliegia," he replied. He knew how to say "cherry" in 38 languages.

"Signore Ciliega. *Sono Teresa.*"

"Of course you are," Cherry replied. "Listen, how'd you like to go to the Caymans for the weekend?"

"Mr. Ciliegia!" She clasped her hands at her breasts as if shocked. Then this little knowing smile, an eyebrow raised. Her hands dropped to her hips, her feet shifted just so. Cherry could smell desire.

He gestured toward the olive-skinned redhead behind the cookie display. "Go get your cousin and meet me at Port Authority," he said. "We'll take the bus."

He watched as she scurried back to the pastry shop, all but tearing off the uniform.

He was crossing Foley Square, the New York Supreme Court Building staring down at him, when he decided to return McHugh's call.

"Francis, I was just—"

"How's LA?"

"Fine, thank you."

McHugh wasn't drinking, he noted. The steel rod was back up her ass.

"His name is Jimmy Gee and he works for Carlos Alvarado," Cherry said as he approached the Brooklyn Bridge. "He copied the data on your cell. Was he worth ten thousand dollars?"

Oh shit. Oh shit. "Francis, I—"

"Forget it," Cherry said. "It'll be a measure of your skill set if he comes back. And by skill set, I mean—"

"I know what you mean, Francis." She was dressing for dinner. The concierge had secured a table at a Spanish restaurant in Beverly Hills. "But he won't be back."

"So…Mary Louise is coming, is she?"

"I'm fairly certain, yes."

"Explain."

"She's run from John Bleak."

That guy. "Say no more," Cherry told her. "I can see it now. A convergence."

He didn't know what to do. He thought about it. He fell asleep on the sofa at the apartment and dreamed about it.

She's gone.

That's it.

She has a new identity.

She'll have a new life.

The Alvarados won't find her.

Cherry will come to his senses.

Amen.

He looked at himself in the mirror.

He was hungry, but he didn't want to leave. She might come back.

He tried to read.

He took another shower.

Call Francis Cherry and tell him where his money is. Tell him she never opened the envelopes.

Call the cops in West Allis and tell them Alvarado killed Kwame Green.

He installed the little alarms.

He put the cell phone on the coffee table and stared at it.

Enter night.

Novel in hand, he looked at the car in the alley.

Prop planes crossed over the San Gabriel Mountains.

The magenta clouds were thin brushstrokes on a black-velvet sky.

He didn't know what to do.

If he'd been sitting on the other side of train in Chicago…

"If," he said to no one.

CHAPTER 15

"Good morning."

McHugh jumped. She hadn't seen him enter the hotel's rooftop deck.

Jimmy Gee nestled on the other side of the table, sliding up onto a stool. He studied McHugh's breakfast, a pineapple half scooped and overflowing with melon. "Looks good."

To one side, a gardener watered pink azaleas. Otherwise, they were alone.

McHugh returned her fork to the mat. She wore a pale-blue shirt, white slacks and gold-trimmed sandals.

Gee pointed a thumb to the carafe near McHugh's iPhone. "Would you mind if I had them bring up an extra cup?"

"It's decaf," she replied.

Huevos rancheros. Black beans. Fresh-baked tortillas. Dodo's boy was sucking on a banana slathered with peanut butter, his paunch hanging over his briefs.

"Where's Quick Draw?" Carlos asked, the scent of diced habanero peppers searing his nose as he entered.

Carmy was in purple again today. "If you mean our brother Fernando, he's sleeping." She tended to a sizzling frying pan.

"Those pills knock him out," Carlos said.

Ignoring the comment, Carmelita said, "Three or four?"

Carlos was thinking of his brother's antiseizure meds. But Carmelita held up a spatula bearing a perfect egg.

His phone chimed as he showed her two fingers.

"Up and at 'em?" Cherry asked.

"I'm having breakfast with my family," Carlos replied. "Family. Do you know the word?"

"Don't be cute, cowboy," Cherry said. "I'm seeing there's a good chance you end it today."

"You're seeing…"

"The girl is missing. She ran off on your ranch-hand bum, and I'm hearing she goes to McHugh."

Carmelita filled her brother's coffee cup, the thought of scalding his balls through his gray suit raising a smile.

Planning his day, Alvarado repeated the hotel name.

"Even if she doesn't turn up, maybe he will. The legendary John Bleak. Big as life. The champ, undefeated in his last two bouts."

"You tell this to Jimmy Gee?"

"I'm telling you," Cherry snapped. "Get the envelope. Put an end to this. Clear?"

Before Alvarado could reply, Cherry cut the connection.

Carmelita slid two glistening eggs on her brother's plate.

"Business," he explained. "It never ends."

"Watch Cesar," she said, nodding toward her grandson as she hurried from the kitchen. Her memory not what it once was, she needed to write down what she heard: Cherry, the hotel, Jimmy Gee…

"Who's Cesar?" Alvarado asked, his mouth dripping yolk.

He slept in fits, his eyelids bobbing as he stretched on the sofa, the paperback tumbling out of his hand. Maybe he was down for two hours, maybe a few minutes more.

He made coffee.

He took a shower, listening for the alarm to sound.

He dressed, wondering where she spent the night.

He planned a quick canvass of the banks he'd visited yesterday. Maybe she turned up at one, retrieved the money and paid a guard to let her walk away without calling him.

He went down to the alley and sat in the car.

He called Chicago. "Hello, my name is Anthony Faithful, and I'm in an embarrassing situation."

He told McHugh's assistant he was a limo driver and his new boss had failed to give him the name of her hotel.

"I'm sorry to bother you with this…"

She threw in the address too.

Thank you.

He called Pup's agent.

"Michael." He saw Koons in linen, Bluetooth headset in his ear, pacing his office, his socks sinking into the carpet. A pile of scripts and a bowl of violet candies on a glass tabletop.

He asked if anyone had tried to contact Pup.

"You can't ask me that," Koons said.

He repeated his new number. "Did I describe the girl?" he asked.

"Please. You're putting me in an untenable position here. No one likes to be cruel…"

"Fernando," Carmelita said over the rushing shower water, "are you all right?"

She had her ear pressed against the door.

"Fernando?"

"All right," he said, his voice stronger than it was yesterday.

"Come out of there, lazy bird. It's time to move."

"Time to move."

She'd sent Cesar to his mother's, calling a limo and charging it to Alvarado Brothers Bail Bonds.

Now she laid his outfit on the bed: a thin blue sweater, navy slacks, sheer black socks, his Smith & Wesson 686, ankle holster, underpants, belt, wallet…

McHugh stared at Gee. He was charming. At least she hadn't been wrong about that.

"How well do you know Cherry?" he asked.

Cherry. Interesting. But she could handle surprises. She'd been point on billion-dollar transactions and always assumed the other side knew everything she'd committed to paper or a hard drive.

"Fairly well," she replied. "We've done business here and there."

"And Szarsynski?"

"She worked for me."

"As—?"

"An admin."

"So she knows your secrets," he said over the lip of his cup.

She tilted her head just so. "Anything anyone else knows is no longer a secret."

Gee returned the cup to its saucer. "Let's clear the air," he said, tugging an earlobe. "The other night… It was fine, right?"

"Maybe better than fine."

He smiled. "I would have said as much. But I don't want it to interfere with what I am about to propose."

She waited. It felt like he was fumbling the play. But she'd been wrong about him before.

"Or maybe the thought is out of line."

"We're fine, Jimmy. We said good-bye. Now it's a different sort of hello."

He wore a black velvet blazer and a black collared shirt. "I can tell you what I've learned and you can tell me what you think I should do."

Be still, she thought. In fact, take that cube of cantaloupe, bring it to your lips, taste it…

"As you know," Gee said, "Cherry hired the Alvarado brothers to find Szarsynski. Now they want me to do it."

"To find her."

"Yes."

"They don't want the job?"

"Her man put them down."

Bleak. John Bleak. "Put them down?"

"Literally. Figuratively too, now that I think about it."

"So they hired you."

"Carlos did." He reached into his pocket and showed her his ID.

"A bail agent?"

"That's what the penal code calls it," Gee replied.

"I don't believe Mary Louise has forfeited a bond in the state of California."

"This is a private matter."

A man with a ponytail was doing laps in the pool. An efficient swimmer, he barely made a sound as he arrowed through candy-blue water.

"Can you negotiate with Cherry?" he asked.

"I have," she replied. "But he is a different sort of beast. It's a blood sport, no doubt."

"You need leverage."

"With Cherry, always."

"Carlos Alvarado killed a man in the pursuit of your former secretary." He told her about Kwame Green.

My goodness, McHugh thought. That is a useful piece of information.

He drove the old Escort with new tires past the boutique hotel. Out front, a valet and a bellman chatted with a woman who was walking her dog. A taxi waited, its engine running. The air conditioner rattled.

Near Melrose Avenue, he stopped and backed the car into a driveway to make a K-turn and head north again.

Maybe Taylor McHugh had already seen Cole. Maybe they spoke. Maybe she's there. Maybe McHugh had influence and told her she'd talk to Cherry and make everything go away.

He waited, a tall hedge blocking traffic that turned off Melrose.

A shining black SUV passed him. Carlos Alvarado was behind the wheel.

She'd taken a bus that ran along Santa Monica Boulevard. When she stepped off, she had a dollar bill, a quarter and two dimes in her pocket.

She didn't know what to do.

She spent the night on a bench by a pier, listening to the Pacific slap the stanchions. Fishermen arrived before dawn.

All that time, the hours ticking, the moon sailing overhead, lizards scooting underfoot, and she still didn't know what to do.

Sam said that Taylor couldn't be trusted.

She was thinking a lot about that. You know, like, what does he know about Taylor?

Well, he knows I was visiting Taylor when that Alvarado guy tried to kill me.

She was the only person who knew I'd be in Chicago.

And Sam said, "Run if you have to, but stay Cole Bennett."

He told me not to use my credit card.

So he was helping me, even after I threatened to see his daughter. Even after I lied to him.

She didn't know what to do. But she was walking downhill toward Taylor's hotel. Dragging, her green flats scuffed on concrete.

"What you're suggesting is," McHugh said, "you'd like to explore the new opportunity."

"Exactly," Gee replied.

"You're thinking greater satisfaction lies with Cherry than with the Alvarado brothers."

"Given the data at hand, it seems probable, yes."

"But you're lacking information," she said. "For example, you don't know why Cherry sent the Alvarados after her."

"Cherry would risk an accessory charge"

"For the murder of Mr. Green?"

"It could go that way."

"Then whatever he wants would have to be something fairly spectacular to justify the exposure, wouldn't you say?"

The pineapple's scent hung between them. The coffee had grown cold.

"Don't tell me you don't know what she has," Gee said.

"I don't know what she has."

Gee sat back. Out of the corner of his eye, he saw the swimmer step from the pool. The gardener was already gone. "I'm not feeling it, Taylor."

"Francis didn't tell me."

"'Francis,' is it?"

"I told him Mary Louise had called me."

"You told him she was coming to Chicago. He told Fernando Alvarado."

"I suppose that's possible, but I hope it isn't the case," she said. "It certainly wasn't my intention to hurt her."

"I wonder if you could be considered an accessory."

She noticed the abrupt change in tone. He was too eager. He'd given more than he'd gotten. He saw a big score and now it was slipping away.

He said, "I think you should broker an introduction. Mr. Francis Cherry and me."

"That might be difficult," she replied. "To be frank, I wouldn't want to do anything to alienate him."

The man who had been swimming had toweled off. He squeezed the water out of his ponytail. Then he wrapped the towel around his trunks and headed to the elevator.

"You'd rather alienate me?"

"Jimmy, why do I have to choose? I don't dispute that you have interesting information, and there's a likelihood that you can leverage it to your advantage."

"I've said that."

"But you can't play Francis Cherry. There's no telling what he will do if he believes he's been crossed."

"Broker the deal." Gee nodded toward her iPhone.

"Did I mention he has an ex-MI-6 operative on retainer?" Pointed to the iPhone this time.

"What's your proposition?"

Gee leaned in. "Tell Cherry about the killing in Wisconsin. Tell Cherry if he's squeezed, Alvarado will claim Cherry told him to do it. Tell Cherry there's a way to ensure that will not happen."

McHugh cleared her throat.

"What?" Gee said.

"I'm not sure you want the benefit of my insight, Jimmy."

"As long as you make the call…"

"What's the endgame? You eliminate a rival, you make a little money, but you're left with Cherry."

His beauty was gone. Oozing greed, he envisioned the life he thought he deserved. She was familiar with his behavior, having seen it many times before. A certain kind of man and there's no such thing as more than often.

She said, "Wherever you think you can take him, he's already been there."

"Well, that may be," Gee said as he stepped off the stool. "But I think this is the way to go."

He looked down at the creases in his black slacks.

"Jimmy, if you want, I'll tell Francis about the killing. I'll recommend that he shift the assignment to you. Let that suffice. OK?"

Gee reached for her hand.

With a sudden jerk, he dislocated her thumb.

McHugh shuddered in shock, her mouth open but silent.

Gee grabbed her wrist. He jiggled her hand until her thumb snapped back into the socket.

He stared hard.

Tears rolled down her cheeks.

"Make the call," he said as he adjusted his jacket.

Carlos Alvarado looked over his steering wheel. He couldn't believe it. He dug into his pocket and looked at a passport-size photo. Woman, photo; photo, woman.

In broad daylight, there was Mary Louise Szarsynski walking down toward the hotel. Walking right toward him.

He reached into his glove box and pulled out his gun.

He decided he'd— Huh? What the fuck?

You got to be kidding me.

His mouth open, he watched as his sister's piece-of-shit Honda drove up and scraped the curb just short of the valet stand.

Carmelita yanked the hand brake and jumped out.

In disbelief, Carlos Alvarado watched as she lumbered around the back to the passenger's side and opened the door for Fernando, who came out slow.

"OK?" said Carmelita.

"OK," Fernando said.

Carlos noticed she'd removed the license plates.

Concentrating, she led Fernando to the back of the car, away from the curious valet.

Carlos saw his sister bend at the knees and remove Fernando's 686 from his ankle holster. She stood and tucked it into the front of his slacks. Then she gently patted his cheek. She ran the back of her fingers along his beard, looking at him with absolute affection.

"Ready?" Carmy asked.

"Ready."

Szarsynski was a half block closer, moving almost as slowly as Fernando.

Carlos tried to think. He didn't get it. Carmelita had sold him out to Cherry? To Gee?

Or maybe she was dealing with McHugh, offering Fernando up as protection against his own brother. She thought like that: let's show Carlito he can't fuck with us. He comes to look for Jimmy Gee, Fernando, and you do like last night, lazy bird, only this time…

Opening the door carefully, Carlos began to climb out of his SUV, looking for a second at the asphalt beneath his feet.

He heard his sister. "Go!" Just like last night.

Carlos dove to the blacktop, covering his head with his arms and hands. When he looked up, he saw Fernando tugging his 686 out of his slacks.

Exiting the hotel, Jimmy Gee turned toward Fernando. He reached beneath his jacket to free his gun.

Racing to hide, the startled valet bumped Gee.

Gee stumbled, his gun crossing his chest as he snapped it from its holster.

Fernando squeezed off a shot and, God damn, it hit Gee in the face between his nose and his upper lip.

Gee collapsed in an instant, slamming the sidewalk.

His blood squirted, a microgeyser.

Up the street, Szarsynski stopped in horror.

"Fernando, let's go," Carmelita said. "Fernando!"

Fernando was stone still, a statue, expressionless. Suddenly, his eyes went wide. Then his back arched violently. Then he started to shake, his head whipping back as a seizure took over his body. The gun tumbled from his hand. He made a gruesome sound that seemed to come from the deepest pit of his being. Then he fell as if flung to the sidewalk. He shuddered and quaked, a fish on a dock. Blood began to pulse from the spot where his head struck concrete.

Carmy panicked. "Fernando!"

Carlos looked toward Szarsynski. She was running up toward Santa Monica Boulevard.

He looked at his sister as she tried to unlock their brother's jaw.

He started running after Szarsynski.

From the side street, he saw Carlos Alvarado step from his SUV, then dive to the ground.

He heard the shot.

Now Alvarado was running past him, past the Escort, a gun in his grip.

He looked and saw Cole Bennett limping as she struggled uphill.

He burst from the car.

He ran.

He saw Alvarado drawing closer to her.

He was gaining on Alvarado.

Zagging into the street, Cole looked over her shoulder. Alvarado was inches away.

Alvarado reached.

He grabbed her by the collar.

He let go as a thunderous blow smashed his tender ribs.

Alvarado dropped in agony.

The man who had assaulted Alvarado in Chicago was on him again.

The man spun him, grabbed him by the sides of his head and pounded it against the street. Twice. A third time, a fourth.

Then he let go and punched him in the center of the face, exploding his nose.

Cole K. Bennett held Alvarado's gun, both fists around the grip.

Panting, Sam said, "Come on."

When she didn't move, he said, "Come on, Cole."

He held out his bloody hand.

She looked over his shoulder. The valet and a bellman were trying to help the woman in purple treat the man on the ground, ignoring the dead man behind them, his blood pooling at the curb.

"The car's here," Sam said.

He yanked her. They hurried downhill to the Escort.

Carmelita Alvarado watched as Fernando stopped quaking. The valet had snapped open his mouth, but the bellman couldn't free his tongue as her brother gagged and choked. "Oh Jesus, help him," she'd shouted in Spanish. She'd blessed herself. Meanwhile, Fernando turned blue. He'd pissed his pants. He died. Right there on the street in West Hollywood.

While Carlos was running away.

She backtracked, her face damp with tears.

Then she rushed to her car. She jumped in, turned over the rattling engine and raced toward Melrose Avenue, sobbing like a child.

CHAPTER 16

McHugh heard sirens, a commotion in the hotel corridor, thudding as people ran by her door. A fire? No alarm… She slipped into shoes, grabbed her purse and rode to the lobby, her thumb encased in an icy facecloth.

She found bedlam in the street, lights whirling on EMS vehicles and police cars. Maybe 50 uniformed personnel were in action. Near the valet stand, a couple of detectives stared down at Jimmy Gee. Blood coated his beautiful face, his glossy hair.

She angled through the milling crowd. Up the block, emergency techs were treating a man. She saw their desperation. He wasn't going to make it either.

On the other side of the street, cops were guarding a black SUV, its driver's-side door open, its engine running. McHugh tried to piece it together. Somebody came after Jimmy Gee. He arrived in that tank over there. He shot Jimmy. Jimmy shot him. Two dead.

She cradled the iPhone in her injured hand. "Ian," she said to Goldsworthy as she walked toward Melrose, her back to the chaos. "You have a major situation out here."

She recited the SUV's license plate number.

Prompted by sirens, Carlos Alvarado came to and rolled under a car at the curb. He stayed there a while, peering around a tire. Despite the agony — he could swear his ribs were ripping through his lungs again — he slid out. He dusted himself off, held a handkerchief to his bleeding nose and staggered uphill toward the boulevard.

Seething, confused, he tried to clear his head and summon the rational man.

Think, he told himself. This is complex. It is rife with emotional issues. Disassociate. Theorize. Here we have a given set of facts.

He turned and backpedaled, looking at the hectic scene, all those cops. Neighbors swarmed. Guests poured from the hotel.

EMS had Fernando under a sheet.

Oh, Jesus Christ.

Fernando.

He shuddered. Tears welled.

But then a wry smile crossed his blood-smeared face.

The last thing you did, Fernando, you took out Jimmy Gee. You went out standing up.

And Carmy. *Cariña*, you got a pair of balls on you.

As for that son-of-a-bitch ranch-hand bum. That coming-up-from-behind son-of-a-bitch bum.

That son of a bitch.

Alvarado hissed and drew up tall.

If it's the last thing I do, I will kill that son of a bitch. He will die in the street just like Fernando.

No. Worse.

He pressed on, breathing shallow through his nose to keep his lungs from inflating. At the chicken joint on the corner, he slipped into the restroom to clean up enough to catch a ride to the Eastside.

He stuffed his nostrils with toilet paper until the blood stopped flowing.

He took out his phone.

Cherry answered.

"Carlos? I hear you're dead."

"Don't be a fool, Cherry. It's your boy Gee."

"I know. You shot him. Like you shot that man in Wisconsin."

In pain, Alvarado struggled for composure. "Didn't you say 'whatever it takes,' Cherry?"

"Not that I recall, no…"

"By the way, Cherry, if you want to give me Fernando's medal for killing Gee, I'll accept it with honor."

"Carlos, listen—"

"As for the future…"

"Carlos—"

"How's this? You come to LA, Cherry. Come to see me scorch the earth. Come see me dice that ranch-hand bum for dog food."

Whoa, thought Cherry, feeling the fury.

"I don't know, Cherry, but I think maybe you want to witness the dismantling of this son of a bitch. Cherry, when you come I promise—"

Alvarado began to cough violently. Blood sprayed the mirror.

He told her to go to the restroom. Freshen up, he said. Remember, we're out here in Pasadena. Nobody knows.

Don't let anybody see you're upset.

He ordered breakfast for her. A salmon omelet with egg whites. A bagel. Maybe you could put some capers on the plate.

Pup liked it that way.

She managed a frail smile as she slid into the booth. "OK?"

He told her she looked exhausted. Which was better than terrified.

"What just happened back there, Sam?"

A thinning out.

"I don't understand."

"Or maybe it's a coincidence that Alvarado was there."

"You don't believe that."

He said he'd find out.

"You think Taylor's involved?"

We've exceeded the limit on the number of times we can claim coincidence.

He said, "What do you think?"

"I think I don't know Taylor McHugh."

The waiter arrived with their meals. He'd ordered a bowl of chicken soup and offered to swap if she wasn't satisfied.

"No, this is great."

He was pleased to see her eat. He'd done the right thing. After all the years he'd worked in the restaurant and food-service industries, it was still pleasing to watch someone enjoy a meal.

She put down her fork. "I'm sorry, Sam. I should've trusted you."

"We're going to have to hide you," he said. "LAPD is in it now."

"Taylor will tell them about me."

Of course.

She sighed.

He told her to take the car back to the apartment. Slip into a long hot bath, get under the covers. Turn off the phone.

"I put an alarm on the door."

She leaned toward him. "And I have his gun," she whispered.

"You know how to use it?"

She said she dated a guy whose idea of a good time was trap shooting.

He took a long sip of the hot soup. Tasted like homemade, the stock simmered long and slowly. He told her he couldn't remember the last time someone cooked for him.

"I miss my mom's cooking," she said. "It's home. You know?"

"I do," he replied, nodding.

McHugh put on a suit and walked to the sheriff's station in West Hollywood. Preemptive contact always suggested maximum cooperation and transparency. Maybe they would respond in kind. She'd report what they said to Goldsworthy.

Soon two detectives arrived. She'd seen them outside the hotel.

She gave them her business card and mentioned she was an attorney.

All right, said the cops.

"How can I help?" she asked.

They were in a sunny conference room off San Vicente Boulevard.

"What happened to your thumb?"

"The man who was shot in front of the hotel damaged it. Dislocated, maybe. I need to see a doctor."

She described him as "a bad bet."

"How so?"

"We dated. It didn't work."

They asked her why she was in Los Angeles.

"I needed to get away. The job's a real bear. I live by myself, my time is my own, I like it out here."

"You can play any way you want."

"There's that, yes."

She told him she met Gee at a restaurant on La Cienega. She conceded that he spent the night. She hadn't expected to see him again. But then…

One of the cops was spinning her card on the tabletop.

"Is there any way you can keep my name out of this?" she asked.

"The hotel," the other cop said. "The valet. The front desk." He stood by the window, hands on his hips.

She nodded and put sorrow in her eyes. "My boss will want an explanation." She was telling them she was going back to Chicago.

"Make up some bullshit," said the cop by the window. "You can pull it off."

"I'm sorry. I don't—"

"Being an attorney and whatnot."

Ad hominem attacks were an admission of anxiety in negotiations.

"It's unfortunate, in any case," she conceded.

"Sure," said the cop seated next to her. "Two dead, right there on a street in a decent neighborhood."

They already knew Gee had spent the night with McHugh, and they'd walked off arm in arm to breakfast the following morning. A waiter said they seemed cozy on the rooftop today, sharing a fruit bowl and a pot of coffee.

They already knew about the rivalry between the Alvarados and Gee.

Maybe the fear of exposure had her throwing her bona fides all over the sheriff's station. Maybe she needed to exert some level of control now that her lover had taken a bullet to his face. Whatever. She didn't shoot anybody.

All right, said the cops. We'll let you know.

She asked the desk sergeant for a tip on a doctor for her thumb. All the while she was thinking how impressed Cherry would be. "Tell them nothing," Goldsworthy said before she entered the station. "Taylor," he said, "if Mr. Cherry is contacted by LAPD—"

"Ian. Please."

She knew what it meant — his tepid threat, the wave of panic in his voice, bodies in the street. Goldsworthy should've handled Mary Louise himself. Decades of decadence and drugs had dulled his edge, so he'd farmed it out. Someone else took on the risk of violence and disaster. But when it blew up, the entire episode flowed through Goldsworthy back to Cherry.

As far as she could see, she was free of blame. She had cooperated with Cherry at every turn.

She asked the desk sergeant if he'd mind calling a taxi. She needed to see a doctor.

The taxi went toward Cedars-Sinai, McHugh examining events from all sides. The chronology: Cherry asks to be told when Mary Louise is in touch; Mary Louise is in touch; she calls Cherry. Assault; death. Really? Her exposure is minimal. What you know versus what you think you know. A quick inventory: data here, bodies there. Is there an axis? Not that I know of. Interpretation trumps fact. There's always an acceptable compromise, a suitable result. An opportunity to be seized.

For the first time since they'd sat across from each other at that steakhouse in Brooklyn as Cherry probed her about life inside the Merc, Taylor McHugh had position. She had room to negotiate.

"Show me how to do it," Alvarado demanded.

The doctor, a tiny man whose father emigrated from Mumbai, said, "Oh, Mr. Alvarado, you know—"

Alvarado stared at him.

Unmoved, Dr. Kini said, "Please. If you would allow me to finish with these bandages—"

Alvarado grabbed a fistful of his hair. He twisted it until Kini's face was pressed flat against the thin paper that stretched across the exam table.

"Get the needles and show me how to do it."

"Mr. Alvarado," Kini grunted, "I cannot be threatened."

By Kini's count, seven people saw Alvarado enter the clinic. They could identify him. He was one memorable piece of damaged humanity.

"I will follow you into your nightmares," Alvarado hissed into the doctor's ear. "Every time you hear creaking steps, it will be me. You'll never spend a day where you won't be looking over your shoulder."

He flung Kini against a row of white cabinets. Everything rattled and rolled.

As Alvarado stared, Kini gathered himself. Adjusting his glasses, he said, "If that is the way it must be, Mr. Alvarado, that is the way it must be."

No fractures, said the X-rays. Kini told him X-rays were unreliable in such cases, and they should treat it as if there was break. The injectable painkiller worked instantly.

Coming off the counter, Kini continued his work, wrapping a bandage around Alvarado's damaged torso.

"Stitches in the back of your head, the bruising in your septum, these terribly, terribly tender ribs…" Kini mused. He was offering Alvarado a way to apologize for his outburst.

"I'm going to kill the son of a bitch who did this."

"Oh I would advise rest. At least for a short while."

"I'm going to kill him now."

"That is the pain talking, I am certain."

Kini hummed while he wrapped his patient, satisfied by the knowledge that he would call LAPD a second after Alvarado limped out of his clinic.

"Write a prescription for the pill version," Alvarado said, looking down.

"That I can do," Kini told him.

"By the way," Alvarado said, "if I hear from LAPD you told some tale on me, I'm going to India and kill your village."

"I was born in Detroit."

"OK. If you want, I'll take out Detroit."

McHugh checked out, avoiding the temptation of one more long, lazy, late afternoon at poolside. She made her way to the limousine the hotel provided. Across the narrow street, a tow trunk lifted a black SUV onto its flatbed, a cop watching the operation.

The 405, the limo driver said, was slow. He suggested La Cienega all the way to LAX.

"That's fine," McHugh said. Her thumb was wrapped tight, holding down the swelling.

She continued making notes, tapping her iPhone with a stylus. Strategizing. Airtight excellence was required to outmaneuver Cherry.

What she must do was becoming more apparent by the moment. There were hourly flights to Chicago or the red-eye east. She had to act fast, but without haste. Whether she would fly home first, directly on to New York, or remain in Los Angeles wasn't yet clear.

She developed a plan of action. Focused on her work, she was surprised when, 30 minutes later, the driver eased to a stop in front of a terminal.

He took the suitcase from the trunk, raised its handle and accepted the tip with a bow and a smile.

She rolled the bag toward a revolving door and paused to enter.

When she came out inside the crowded terminal, she stopped and looked for a place to work while she gave body to her plan.

"There's a brew pub," said John Bleak, as he stepped beside her.

He wore a blue blazer, a crisp white oxford, jeans and running shoes. The clothes seemed new, like he'd bought them moments ago. His sandy hair was a mop, and his eyes sagged, but she saw he was scrubbed clean and shaved.

A damaged man, though. She hadn't noticed that when he came to her in her office.

"The end begins here," John Bleak said.

"I agree," McHugh replied. "We begin the end."

CHAPTER 17

The bar was crowded with travelers, but they'd found a dark corner. A stock ticker scrolled across every TV screen. Back in New York, the market had closed. The Dow blah-blah, the S&P 500 blah-blah-blah…

She ordered the ahi salad. He asked for the iceberg wedge, hold the blue cheese and bacon. He used to take a lot of heat for that, iceberg lettuce. When he worked in a world of mizuna, mâche and tat soi, he preferred its directness, its crunch. Pup said it tasted like wet air.

The waiter really wanted them to buy beer, but McHugh declined with such condescension that the guy went away without asking her guest what he'd like to drink.

He saw she'd changed from the meeting in her office.

She had a hand to play.

"Do you know what happened at the hotel?" she asked.

Yes.

"And so you know it all started with Mary Louise."

He said, "It started with Alvarado assaulting her."

"If she hadn't—"

"You want to gloss over that?"

She said, "The point is, is she hadn't—"

"You knew she had it. You could've helped her—"

"If she hadn't taken it," McHugh said, raising her voice, "none of this would've happened."

"She made a mistake. She came to you for help. She was coming to you today when Gee was shot."

"Because she no longer trusts *you*."

"She doesn't know who to trust." He leaned and scratched his back against the chair's rail. The shirt wouldn't sit right. He couldn't get his usual brand; they didn't have six in his size. Instead, he went into a big-man's shop and he bought the smallest shirt he could find. At a drugstore he bought a bar of oatmeal soap and washed in a men's room, stripping down to his shorts, scouring like he wanted to wear away his skin. He'd been on the road a long time.

"Well, I would suggest she choose someone," McHugh said. "People are killing each other."

"What can you do for her?"

"I think I can prevent her from being the next body on the sidewalk, Mr. Bleak."

"OK. Do it."

"But it's not as simple as it sounds."

He said, "She'll return what she took. But he has to let her walk away."

"He won't do that."

"If he wants what she has, he'll have to."

"You don't understand," McHugh said. "The money doesn't matter."

To someone like Cherry? True.

"He wants her. She's made him look weak. Even if she hands him every cent she took, he won't be satisfied."

"She has more than his money."

"If she— What?"

He said, "You don't know what she has, do you?"

He waited.

"Do you?" she asked.

He waited.

"Will you tell me what she has?"

"I'll give you what she has," he said. "But she has to be allowed to disappear."

"I can't promise that."

"I think you can," he said. "I think you can tell Mr. Cherry you'll give him what he wants if he lets her go."

"And I should bring it back to him? Whatever it is?"

He watched as McHugh paused to think.

"Regardless of who returns it, he'll never forget."

"He doesn't have to forget," he said. "He has to say he won't touch her."

"Mary Louise told you to make this offer?"

There is no Mary Louise.

"I need to think about it," McHugh said.

He stood, sliding back his chair as the waiter arrived with their meal.

She called after him. "Mr. Bleak. John."

He edged through the mass at the bar, stepping over luggage, avoiding a waitress with a loaded tray.

Standing, McHugh watched as he disappeared into the crowded terminal.

Rush-hour traffic crawled on the 110. Brake lights flashed as cars lingered for miles. A minor accident at the 101 cutoff dammed the freeway. Palm trees at the roadside seemed to sag in defeat.

But he felt fine. He could see it now. He was getting her out of it. He didn't know what he was doing, but he was doing all right.

Two hours after he left LAX, he pulled the rental behind the Escort.

He called from the alley.

"I'm coming up," he said.

He didn't want to frighten her. He didn't want the alarm to blare.

"OK. Good," she said.

He opened the door. He was greeted by a remarkable scent.

And there she was, Cole K. Bennett, a wide smile on her face, all sorts of refreshed in a pale T and jeans, a towel in her hands.

"I made dinner."

He didn't know what to say.

"Welcome home, Sam."

Meatloaf with baked potatoes, green beans and a salad.

She stared at him as he ate.

"Happy?"

His mouth full, he nodded.

"We're meat-and-potatoes girls, my mom and me," she explained.

"Lucky me."

"Ketchup?"

"Doesn't need it."

"Another beer?"

"Not yet," he said.

She had an appetite too. Her potato was almost gone, a little puddle of butter in its place.

"Tell me something about yourself," she said.

"I like meatloaf."

"No kidding," she said as she pointed a folk toward his plate. "But I mean something for real."

"For real. I like meatloaf."

"Like what do you do for a living?"

He said, "More jobs than I can count."

"Like?"

"Like whatever I could grab."

"Sam…"

"Delivered pizzas, worked a loading dock, security at a railroad yard, at a convention center. Pumped gas. Hauled lumber, hauled rubber. Made keys. Drove a Strick. Had a hack license for a while."

"No career?"

"Not until the CIA," he said as he speared his green beans.

"The CIA?" She put down her fork. "Well, I can't say I'm surprised."

"In St. Helena and Hyde Park."

"Wait. I thought the CIA—"

He said, "The Culinary Institute of America."

"The Culinary—"

"The CIA. And I swear to you I never made a meatloaf as good as this."

She began another question, but he put a finger across his lips.

When he nudged her to take seconds, she said, "Let's have sandwiches tomorrow. Cold meatloaf is the best."

A cold meatloaf sandwich on the road. Good.

"You're leaving tomorrow," he said.

"I'm leaving for where?"

"Start back toward Wisconsin."

"I don't understand."

"I think you're out of this."

He spooned more green beans onto his plate. When he offered her the bowl, she shook her head.

"I talked to McHugh. She's going to contact Cherry."

"I thought we didn't trust her."

He shrugged.

She sat back and folded her arms. "Do we?"

He sipped the cold beer. "This has gotten way out of hand. Murder. Bodies. Who wants this? Nobody. Let's let her give him the envelopes and everybody moves on."

"Just like that."

Just like that.

"You don't know these people."

He said, "I'll call Cherry and tell her McHugh has it. I'll tell him nobody knows he hired the Alvarado brothers. Maybe he'll see it's best if it stays that way."

They sat in silence.

"So that's it," she said as she lifted her beer. "I go and everything's forgotten."

"I don't know about that. Maybe you're Cole Bennett for a while."

"And what happens to you?"

I go and everything's forgotten.

He held out his hand.

Alvarado couldn't sleep, though the painkillers dulled his mind.

He went down to the lobby and got the guy vacuuming the carpet to let him take Cuervo Gold up to bed.

Three o'clock, 3:30. Four.

He woke hours later in a heavy fog, sun streaming through the windows.

He moaned.

His head. His ribs.

His phone was buzzing like a motherfucker, and he'd forgotten he'd spent the night ignoring it.

"Yeah." His voice a coarse bleat. He was naked except for his shoes and the wrap around his ribs.

"Carlos Alvarado?"

Blood on the bedspread. His nose bled during the night.

"What?"

"My name is Taylor McHugh."

He tried to stand, but the room spun.

Then the world landed on him. Fernando was dead.

Oh, that ranch-hand son of a bitch.

"Mr. Alvarado?"

"What?"

"Perhaps this is a bad time."

"What do you want?" He put his hand on the nightstand.

"I have a proposition for you. It involves Francis Cherry. I believe you may hold him responsible for the death of your brother."

He gave her the name of the hotel.

He said, "If you bring the police, I will dismember everyone in your family."

"Now why would you want to do that, Mr. Alvarado?"

"To satisfy a primal urge."

"Really?" she said. "It's nothing more than that?"

His head spinning, Alvarado replied, "It's nothing less than that, Taylor McHugh."

"At any rate, you'll have to take it up with Mr. Cherry."

"Oh, I intend to do that too," Alvarado said. "Tell me, does he have a family I can eviscerate?"

He knocked on Cole's bedroom door.

"Can you be ready in a half hour?"

She took a shower, the bathroom already warm and moist, the scent of his shaving cream in the air.

"Sam, did you sleep?"

They went to the bank.

The security guard saw them walk in together. The guard nodded. She's back. Nice going.

They went down to the vault. The money was still in the envelope. So were the other two smaller envelopes. As she said, neither had been opened.

He told her to take $5,000.

"What about you?" she said.

I'm fine.

She handed him the package. He tapped it on the shelf, settling the bills.

"So this is it. I'll never see you again?"

He shook his head.

Her lip fluttered a bit. "You know, my father died when—"

"Please," he said. "You're going to shine. Believe it." It takes more than one mistake to ruin a life.

She said, "Hold me, Sam."

Oh Jesus.

He walked her to the car.

"Take the Two-ten to Fifteen north."

He put a note in the sack that held her sandwich. You're going to have to be alone for a while, he wrote. But you'll be all right.

He watched the car disappear.

He went back to the room and took a shower.

His shirts were ready at the laundry.

Cherry was having brunch in a French bakery on Grand Street, one in a chain that prided itself on fresh bread and communal dining. His back was to the room. From what he could hear, a conference of affected assholes was underway. They bitched about the crush of traffic to the Hamptons, the cost of Filipino housekeepers and Irish nannies, and how they'd already spent their bonuses on necessities like sable bath mats, golf camp in St. Andrews and high colonics. They needed brioche and mochaccinos before they could face a world that denied them cradle-to-grave mother's milk. If he had to go to war with these whiny fucks, he'd pull the pin and hold the grenade to his chest as soon as he hit sand.

"Everything you told me is wrong," he said into his cell.

"I'm sorry, Francis. But it was chaos."

Quoting Goldsworthy's report from memory, he said, "It wasn't Carlos. It was Fernando. He wasn't shot. He had a seizure." Then he added, "Your boyfriend took one from a half-wit. A noodle."

"Francis, we have to talk."

He stood and dropped a $20 bill on top of his copy of Barron's. That should cover the coffee and toast.

"I can get your goods for you. But I have to pay."

Cherry elbowed through the crowd. A guy who worked at Towers Perrin stared, his mouth open, slice of spelt hanging in midair. He'd told Cherry about a company's move on its aerospace rival over rib eyes and an '82 Petrus. Cherry shorted the stock, told a semirespected blogger about the takeover and pointed out the company was buying debt and not much innovative. In four hours, Cherry made $3.8 million. Fuck the SEC.

"Pay what?" He was on Grand Street now, the Soho cobblestone still damp from last night's cloudburst.

"I can get it."

"What is 'it,' Taylor?"

"You'll have to tell me. Francis, please, now is not the time to be cute."

"'It' is an envelope. Inside, there's cash and two other envelopes."

"I assume the two envelopes—"

"Taylor, don't assume. There are worse men in the world than Carlos Alvarado and the late Jimmy Gee."

"Do I have your authorization—"

"Use the cash in the envelope. Front the rest."

McHugh said, "There's a limit to how much I can cover."

"Taylor, I know exactly how much you can raise. You dip on every deal you bring me out of your shop."

She said she'd be in touch.

"Don't touch. Get it, get on a plane, be in my office."

"Francis—"

"Do I have to tell Alvarado to check up on you?"

"Let the man grieve," McHugh said. "He's lost a brother."

He looked at her room. He went out to the sofa and slept.

It was dark when he woke up. He'd lost a day.

Good.

He needed to disengage.

He couldn't wait to be lost again.

He went to the refrigerator. Under plastic wrap, meatloaf on a platter and a shriveled baked potato. Three beers. The rest of the food she'd bought.

She was going to make this place a home.

He'd had a home but he lost it. He could've insisted. He could've demanded. You don't have to testify, Moira. Let them come after me.

You don't have to prove anything to me. What I did, that's on me, not you.

He had to get out.

He opened a shirt and hung it on the back of a chair.

He took off his jeans, pulled off his socks.

He needed a shower. The water's roar would drown out the sound of Pup's voice.

No it wouldn't.

It was nighttime now. He had to move.

LA had a light rail system. He'd never been on it.

You could go as far south as Long Beach.

Maybe he'd walk along the ocean, listen to the surf pound, watch the stars over the Pacific. He couldn't count the times he'd slept on a beach.

He'd fallen out of habit. His mind was active again. He was feeling. He knew he'd see Moira's footprints in the sand. He'd see Pup, two years old and studying a seashell.

He looked out the window. There was an empty space in front of his rental car.

He wondered if Cole K. Bennett was all right.

Maybe she was in Nevada. Maybe she was spending the night in Vegas. A lark.

Knowing her now and how Kwame Green stood vivid in her mind, no.

He ran his fingers through his hair and wiped the sleep from his eyes.

His phone rang, and he worried it was her.

Taylor McHugh told him to be in Griffith Park at 6 a.m. "At the merry-go-round."

"Why?"

"To give me the package to bring to Cherry."

"Why not now?"

"Please," she said. "It's been a very trying day."

CHAPTER 18

He drove all night. Pasadena down to Santa Ana. Santa Ana over to Torrance. Torrance up to Sherman Oaks, taking Sepulveda and crawling past police action following a drive-by, a sleeping six-year-old girl killed in a car outside a club, klieg lights, news crews. He bought coffee and a doughnut before climbing Mulholland. He arrived at Griffith Park at 4 a.m., entering at the Greek Theatre and winding north. He parked near a picnic area.

He waited.

The moon tumbled toward the ocean.

He expected early hikers or birders. A photographer, maybe. But nothing until almost 5 a.m., when a park ranger drove by.

At 5:30, the glow before sunrise.

He walked toward the merry-go-round, its red-and-white canopy draping rearing horses in heavy shadows, a ghostly stampede.

When she was a child wearing Oshkosh overalls, Pup rode a jumper in Central Park. He shot a video on a bulky camera. Calliope music played.

Daisy, Daisy, give me your answer do. I'm half crazy, all for the love of you.

Moira snuck away from the U.S. marshals so she could retrieve the video. It was in her desk at school. She taught third grade. Her killer was waiting, the second-generation thug. I found her, the marshals and NYPD running behind. I saw the blood on the wall before I saw her body.

A car came up the drive and passed the park headquarters.

It pulled into the lot, its lights sweeping the dense trees.

Taylor McHugh was alone.

He was on a bench behind a row of thick bushes.

The envelope was tucked into the back of his pants. Tail feathers when he was seated. Now it was well concealed under his blazer.

McHugh waved at him.

Old friends.

She wore pressed jeans and a thin sunflower sweater over a coral T. Gold earrings and a matching bracelet.

She had a bandage on her thumb. The valet said she was fine when her breakfast with Jimmy Gee began, but she'd come out with it wet-wrapped after he'd been shot and killed.

Maybe she contacted the Alvarados to take care of their rival. Maybe she hadn't called them to pick up Cole.

Maybe she hadn't called Cherry and told her Mary Louise Szarsynski was going to visit her in Chicago.

Maybe she didn't know Fernando Alvarado tried to kill Mary Louise in the parking garage.

He didn't care anymore.

He wanted them to leave her alone.

Then he wanted to exit California and disappear.

McHugh said, "I apologize for the cloak and dagger—"

He pointed to a security camera near the ride.

There were three empty patrol cars in the headquarters lot.

With the sun glowing to the east, hikers were preparing to mount Beacon Hill. Golfers were queuing at Wilson and Harding, coffee containers in hand.

"When I was a boy, I saw a woman fall off a carousel. She landed right at my feet and I didn't do a damned thing. I walked away."

"Mr. Bleak."

"Why did you set her up?"

"I don't understand."

"Your former secretary. She's a good kid."

"Francis Cherry would say she's a thief."

"Tell me about him."

"I don't think I will. No."

He held up three fingers. "Three dead."

"Aren't we here to put an end to all that?"

I don't know.

"Do you have the envelope?"

He said yes.

"Well…"

"I want your word."

"Mr. Bleak."

He looked at her. Her expression never changed.

Death. Lives ruined. For Taylor McHugh, all good things. Opportunities.

She said, "I'm flying to New York—"

He knew she had acted only out of self-interest. She traveled to LA because she knew Cole would come to her. She saw Cole as irrelevant. For a fee, she would take the envelope and return it to Cherry. Whether Cole took another beating or whether another good man like Kwame Green was killed didn't matter. She wanted her reward, her commission.

"In three hours. Francis Cherry expects me to deliver the envelope."

"She's a good kid."

"If you want me to concede that I was surprised when I heard she'd done this, I will."

"He'll leave her alone."

"That's our goal, isn't it?"

"He'll leave her alone. Or I will come for you."

She stared up at him.

He reached and slipped the envelope from under his blazer.

He handed it to her.

She opened the flap.

"How much?"

"About fifty thousand. I didn't count."

She rummaged through the bills, all in thin, orderly packs, until she found the two smaller envelopes.

"They're sealed," he said, as she inspected them. "Cherry knows his envelopes were sealed."

"I don't believe you have any idea what Francis Cherry knows."

Again, he pointed to the camera above the merry-go-round. "If he can access GPS technology to locate a cell…"

"Yes. It's best I deliver this to him as quickly as possible."

"Tell me you didn't walk her into an ambush."

"In Chicago?"

At the hotel in West Hollywood.

"Did you call the Alvarados to your hotel?"

"Good-bye, Mr. Bleak."

Dismissed, he watched as she walked away.

"She's a good kid," he repeated.

She turned. "That may be so. But she did something that upset Francis Cherry." She waved the envelope. "It made him very angry."

He came out the way he came in and got on the 5 heading south toward downtown. He wasn't sure what he was going to do.

It felt like he could stick around a while longer, the job done, Cole K. Bennett on her way. He could go to Century City, talk to Michael Koons, tell him Pup was out of danger. Relieved, Koons would tell him something she'd said. He could ask, How is she, Michael? Is she all right?

Traffic was light. He was going to be near Union Station before he knew his next move.

Maybe back to Pasadena to sleep, the cheap cell on the coffee table.

A meatloaf sandwich for breakfast.

He smiled.

"Cold meatloaf is the best."

He felt the car tugging to the right.

Like the Escort before he had it fixed.

He signaled and moved to the right lane.

No shoulder.

He got off the freeway and eased to the roadside.

A flat tire.

He stared at it.

He couldn't remember how many rental cars he'd left on the side of the road, in NO LOADING zones, in parking lots, outside airport terminals.

Hands on his head, he looked around and saw, a block or two away, a truck lot. Dozens of baby-blue vehicles were at rest on a Sunday.

He thought maybe somebody could lend him better than a sub-compact jack, a thin aluminum crank that was always hell to work.

Then he'd be back on the road, riding on a doughnut spare.

Or to hell with it. Maybe he'd walk until he didn't want to walk anymore.

Or drive to Westwood and see Pup, if only from a distance. He'd park in the shadows. He'd peer around trees. Five minutes, not a second more.

He took off his blazer and tossed it on the backseat. The gun was in a side pocket.

He rolled up his sleeves.

It was going to be a beautiful day. Wispy clouds lazed in the tranquil sky. He was 20 miles from the beach, but he could hear the surf, feel the sand, the sun massaging his tired body.

He opened the trunk.

Carlos Alvarado sprang out, his teeth gritted, eyes wild.

He stun-gunned him, pressing it against his chest.

Two million volts of electricity roared through his body.

While he screamed and rattled, Alvarado snapped plasticuffs around his wrists and shoved him into the trunk, slamming down the lid as he tumbled.

Hissing in pain, Alvarado wriggled behind the steering wheel and took the limping car to a side street.

He parked. He went back to the trunk.

He had the son of a bitch who attacked him twice. The son of a bitch who destroyed Fernando. Who made him a fool.

Look. The son of a bitch was trying to regain his senses.

With a crisp backhand slap, Alvarado slugged him with a leather blackjack, knocking him out.

"That is how a professional does it," he said to no one, as he retrieved his foam sealant for the flat.

Driving west now on the Santa Monica Freeway, Alvarado realized he hadn't taken down a runner by himself in maybe five or six years, maybe more. More.

This guy, this son of a bitch, he locked him up in less than 10 seconds. In broad daylight, despite the relentless agony in his torso, the blood in his piss, the ache in his heart.

His brother would've been proud.

When I claim your body, *mijo*, I'll tell you what I did.

CHAPTER 19

Alvarado parked in the scoop in front of his house.

The son of a bitch in the trunk was awake, but he was hurting.

"Get out."

He got out slowly, swinging his long legs.

Courtesy of the plasticuffs Alvarado clipped around his wrists, his hands were swollen and purple, veins throbbing. A lump was forming on his head.

He steadied himself on the back bumper, fearing he'd fall face-first onto adobe slate.

That stun gun hurt like nothing he'd ever felt before, like maybe his blood boiled and he was ready to pop. He looked down and saw a little burn mark in his cotton shirt that said nothing about the pain.

"And don't think the cops are coming to rescue you," Alvarado said as he pushed him toward the front steps. "I told them I would be in on Monday. They're all right with that. 'Whatever, Mr. Alvarado.' They got no problem with me. They *respect* me."

Alvarado saw his brother, strong and fit. Then he saw his brother with his eyes emptied, the light dimmed.

He saw himself as he used to be.

He punched the son of a bitch in the ribs, a roundhouse launched from behind.

Throwing it made Alvarado's body sting to his spine, but he took satisfaction at seeing the son of a bitch drop to his knees.

"Up," he said.

The man tried to crawl.

"Hey, son of a bitch. Up."

Alvarado didn't have the strength to carry him into the living room. For a moment, he thought about beating him to death right here under God's golden sun.

Alvarado used the leather blackjack with terrifying efficiency, raising it slowly, snapping it gently and cracking it against knees, elbows, ankles. One blow to the femur made the ranch-hand bum's entire body numb. He'd already passed out twice.

Alvarado was washing down his painkillers with tequila.

He'd stripped to his boxers, he tore off the bandages. His body glistening with sweat, his midsection a riot of yellow and purple bruises.

An hour ago, maybe two, maybe three, Alvarado had cuffed him to a chair he'd dragged in from the kitchen, plasticuffed his wrists behind him, tied his ankles to the chair's legs.

"What you did," Alvarado said as he kicked over his coffee table.

Raw sunlight blasted through thin curtains. Palm trees stood sentry.

It occurred to him that he was going to die.

"What you did," Alvarado repeated.

The gag ripped his mouth at the corners.

He bled from his ear. A blood-filled mouse rose above his left eye.

Alvarado circled him, searching for unmarked places to strike.

Circled. Circled.

He panted, hissed and groaned.

"We worked and we worked and we worked, son of a bitch."

He sapped him on his neck near the collarbone.

"And it was a pleasure."

Then on the other side.

"You know why? Because Fernando was the best," Alvarado said as he circled. "You told him to do something, and something got done. Never did you have to tell him twice."

Now he had the bottle of tequila in his fist. He took a slug. He wiped his lips with the bare forearm.

"Me, I lost my way. Not Fernando. This was a man who knew why he was born."

He hit the son of a bitch square on the bridge of the nose. Blood spurted onto his shirtfront.

The man cuffed to the chair began to cough. He was having troubling breathing. There was no place he didn't hurt.

He was an open wound.

He knew he was finally getting what he deserved.

Alvarado said, "You ask Fernando about the job and he would make a face, just a little change in expression, and you know what? He was telling you the job was done."

The coughing wouldn't stop. He couldn't breathe. The room spun. He thought he saw something.

Alvarado tapped him again, this time on the kneecap.

He took another mouthful. He sprayed the son of a bitch with tequila.

"You tell me. Tell me. Where am I going to find a mechanic like that? A man that can do his job like a man. Tell me."

His head bobbed. He was going to pass out.

Alvarado grabbed his hair and lifted his head.

He stepped in until their noses touched. "You fuck with me, *chingado*. You fuck with my coin, I fuck with you. Look at me. Look at me! We're going do this all day. You, I'm taking apart piece by piece. First I tenderize you some more, and then I take you apart."

Alvarado let go of the man's head and moved back. He brought his arm wide. The sap was going to catch the son of a bitch on the jaw and snap it off its hinges.

"You fuck with my business, you—"

A gunshot.

Alvarado lurched into him, then bounced off. He landed on the bloodstained carpet with a thud, dead before the next heartbeat.

Through bleary eyes, the man cuffed to the chair saw a stout woman in a purple jumpsuit.

She'd put a bullet into the back of Alvarado's head.

She walked over. She looked down at his body, her expression rigid with rage.

She leaned over and spit on the dead man's face.

He didn't know what happened. He couldn't see clearly. He couldn't understand. He heard her voice. She was talking to a corpse.

"Fernando was more than an employee," she insisted. "He was not a killing machine. He was our brother. "And you gave him up like nobody would give up a dog," she said, screaming now.

He passed out again.

He woke up on the floor, his hands free, but his ankles still tied to the chair.

Alvarado lay next to him.

Maybe it was late afternoon.

It took him a while to crawl to the kitchen, the chair dragging behind him, and cut himself free.

He stood and the room spun.

Whoa.

He groped to steady himself against a counter.

He turned on the cold water and stuck his head into the sink.

He watched his blood spiral down the drain.

Maybe he was alone.

Maybe the woman who shot Alvarado was gone.

He stumbled to a small bathroom in the corridor.

He looked in the cabinet mirror.

Oh Jesus.

He did the best he could, dabbing with a facecloth, dabbing with peroxide, but it was useless. He was a mess. Maybe he could get by without stitches, but the swelling was a nightmare, his face and body a gruesome rainbow.

He let go of the sink and stood tall.

When he breathed, there was a rattle deep in his chest.

He dug the keys out of Alvarado's pocket.

He stepped outside. The dull evening light blinded him.

In agony, he inflated the tire again with foam.

He drove toward Pasadena, straining to stay steady.

His head bobbed.

On the 110, he opened the glove compartment and took out his cell phone.

Nobody called.

The freeway was a blur.

He needed help.

Desperate to stay alert, he calculated.

Pup was only 25 miles away.

Pup was a world away minus 25 miles.

In a fast-food parking lot, he passed out behind the wheel. When he woke up, it was night, stars were scattered overhead.

The same stars that looked down on Westwood, and wherever Cole K. Bennett might be.

CHAPTER 20

They were lava-flowing out of the subway, careening down Wall Street from Broadway, streaming up from the east, zombie-eyed, not yet zoned for the flood of numbers and nonsense. Away for a moment from the workers' parade into the financial district, Taylor McHugh stood over by the old Morgan Bank. Jet-lagged — her body knew it should still be nestled in bed in West Hollywood — she paused to gather her thoughts. A joyless line snaked from a coffee wagon. The flag on the facade of the stock exchange needed a steam cleaning.

The air was sauna thick. It was going to rain today. A summer downpour. Before they bounced, raindrops would vaporize. Here, gone.

Slanting through the crowd, she walked along Broad Street on the shady side to the U.S. headquarters of Francis Cherry Investment Counseling.

An armed guard studied her ID. He handed her a pass. Ten steps later, she showed it to another guard, who used his badge to open a glass gate.

Upstairs, she looked for Goldsworthy at reception, but he wasn't there to meet her.

He doesn't know what's in the envelopes either, she thought, and Cherry doesn't want him to know.

A senator's son in seersucker and a bowtie escorted her along the carpeted hall.

"Nice tan," said Francis Cherry as she entered the office.

"July in LA, Francis. You catch a tan strolling to the car."

"I'm sure that's it," he replied. The Hang Seng was flat all day, up an eighth, down an eighth. Perfectly hedged, he was ready to pounce, but nothing moved.

She was dressed appropriately for a de facto job interview, back in the blue suit she had on when she was interviewed by LAPD. This morning, she augmented it with the scarf she wore the night she met Jimmy Gee.

Cherry pointed to a leather chair.

"Quite an adventure, Francis," she said as she settled in.

"Give."

"Of course. But—"

"Before you 'but,' remind me: Did I mention there are worse men than Carlos Alvarado and Jimmy Gee?"

"Francis, there's no need."

The threat evaporated. She knew she'd done well. She'd managed his crisis, and Cherry was going to reward her by bringing her back to New York. He'd install her in a senior post at Cherry Counseling, maybe let her open a new branch of Cerasus, advising on mergers and acquisitions. Seven-figure salary, points, open-ended expense account, penthouse on the Upper East Side, chauffeur…

Outside, storm clouds threatened Wall Street.

She said, "How much did you have to begin with?"

"Cash? Who the fuck knows. Cash…" he spit.

"I gave what was left to Alvarado. Forty-seven thousand, five hundred dollars."

"Give. Me. The. Envelope."

Since all the cash was gone, it folded easily into her purse, the two smaller envelopes tucked safely inside.

He unfolded it, turned it over and shook the two envelopes onto his desktop.

McHugh thought she saw him sigh in relief.

Cherry dug out an ivory-handled letter opener and slit an envelope's seal.

Squeezing it, he peered inside.

Then he stared at McHugh.

She leaned toward him. "Francis?"

The other envelope was empty too.

He wasn't doing well.

He wobbled to the bathroom and vomited, though he hadn't eaten in more than 24 hours.

He'd iced his bumps and bruises one at a time, to little effect.

He tried to pinch his wounds to staunch the bleeding, but they trickled and refused to scab.

He felt his head might burst.

Nobody called.

He took the elevator down to the car and drove to an all-night drugstore, the clerks recoiling as he filled a handbasket with supplies.

He trembled when he walked.

At a gas station, he bought all the ice they had in the chest. The guy behind bulletproof glass started to say something, but the hunched, limping man with swollen eyes and bruises held up his hand.

Back at the apartment building, he loaded the elevator. The trip to and from the car, to and from the car, took forever.

He filled the bathtub with ice and cold water. He lowered himself into the tub and stayed there until the ice melted and his lips had gone blue.

He poured peroxide on his wounds. When the hissing stopped, he applied butterfly bandages.

He realized he'd lost four teeth.

He stood naked in the living room and, feeling faint, took inventory, running his mind up and down his body.

Finally, he decided nothing was broken.

He was going to be all right.

"He told me they were in there," McHugh said quickly.

"Who's he?"

"Carlos Alvarado."

"When?"

"Yesterday."

Cherry was pacing. McHugh turned in the chair to follow him.

"From the beginning…" he said.

"Mary Louise was coming to me and her guy, John Bleak, was with her."

"Like that? In broad daylight?"

"No. Not until Jimmy Gee was shot. Then he ran out. Maybe Alvarado was following them."

Cherry dipped his head and stared at her from under an arched brow.

"I'm getting this secondhand, Francis. Remember, I was upstairs." She showed him the bandage on her thumb.

The gray sky rumbled low and deep.

"Go on."

"Alvarado grabbed her and Bleak jumped in. I guess they negotiated."

"'Negotiated.'"

"Negotiated. The envelope for her release," she said, fighting panic. "Alvarado."

"A trade. Ah."

"I didn't want to know the details, Francis." She was standing now too.

"So Alvarado comes to your hotel with the envelope. He comes to your room. He gives you the envelope. You give him the cash."

"Forty seven thousand, five hundred."

"You shake hands. Everything's sweet."

"I had your goods."

"He walks out happy."

"I wouldn't say happy. The job was over, and he was paid."

"Transaction complete."

She took a deep breath. "Apparently not."

"His brother is dead on the sidewalk, but he's negotiating."

She staggered. "Francis—"

"The cops are looking for him, but he strolls up to your hotel."

"Francis, I can explain."

He walked toward his view to Broad Street.

A thunderclap exploded. McHugh jumped.

Rain in windy sheets swept across Cherry's windows.

He was asleep. The phone rang. He moaned.

"Sam, I'm in Denver," she said. "Sam? Are you all right?"

He tried to speak.

"Sam?"

"Cole."

"What happened?"

"No," he said. "We're good. It's fine."

"You sound funny."

His lips were bloated. He hadn't learned to work around his missing side teeth.

"I was sleeping."

"Yes. And—?"

"I'm all right. Alvarado's gone. Dead."

"Sam. Did you—"

"Not me. No."

"Something happened," she said.

Yes. Something happened.

"I wish I was there, Sam. I'd take care of you."

He sighed.

"Sam, can I go home?"

He cleared his throat. "Where's home?"

"With my family."

He'd put a top sheet on the sofa. It was dotted with blood.

He told her to check in at a hotel near Union Station in Denver. He mentioned the chain where she stayed in Chicago.

"Maybe I should come back," she offered.

No.

"I'm leaving California," he told her.

He stood slowly, his muscles taut and battered.

"How's the car?" he asked as he tottered toward the kitchen. "It's not shimmying too much, is it?"

Cherry knew what happened to Carlos Alvarado. According to Goldsworthy, everybody in Los Angeles County knew. He was found dead, shot in his home. A rivalry between bail bondsmen said one of the TV reporters camped outside the house. That made no sense to Cherry, but what the hell. Maybe the cops wanted it to end that way, three licensed shitheels off the street if you include Fernando. Maybe he was out of it too. Almost.

Cherry told her Alvarado was dead.

"John Bleak," she said.

He was sitting next to McHugh now, perched on the chair's arm. The rain continued to rattle the windows.

"John Bleak," she repeated. "He killed Alvarado."

"Well, it was somebody. The ghost of Jimmy Gee? The ghost of Kwame Green?"

"You know about Kwame?"

"Was that your play, Taylor? Pinning Green to me?"

"I didn't say that."

"Maybe you killed Alvarado."

"It was Bleak. He has your money and the envelopes."

"Taylor," Cherry said. "You have the money. You put it in your hotel safe this morning."

"I did not—"

"Want to see the footage?"

"That money—"

"Do you have the envelopes?"

"Francis."

Cherry held up a finger. "You're in the middle of a thing, Taylor. A bad thing."

"I—"

"See, Taylor, if Carlos Alvarado had a moment alone with this John Bleak, he would've set out to turn his bones to dust." He snapped a hand in front of her face. "He wanted his eyes for dice."

McHugh opened her mouth, but nothing came out.

"And yet Alvarado is dead. And John Bleak is alive. And he knows where you live. And he believes you are responsible for what happened to Mary Louise."

Cherry stood.

"Hoo boy. What a fix. But worse for you, no?"

The phone rang on his desk.

Francis Cherry said, "Sure. Put him through."

Cherry listened, then pressed the mouthpiece against his shoulder.

"It's John Bleak," he said. "Want me to tell him you're here?"

Four days later, he put on a pair of sunglasses and went downtown to the train station. Walking slowly, he bought six paperbacks and a ticket. LA to Chicago, Chicago to Washington, Washington to Philadelphia. Three days on trains. In private roomettes for most of the trip. They brought his meals to him. He showered down the corridor.

He slept, and when he wasn't sleeping, he was reading.

His body mended.

Nobody called him.

He walked through Chicago's Union Station in search of a bookstore and a barbershop.

Was he here only last week? Seemed longer than that.

Cole Bennett made time matter again.

He was going to work hard to forget her.

But he knew he could do it.

Wasn't like she was Moira. Or Pup.

Wasn't like she stood on the line between then and now.

Cherry suggested they meet in his office.

A Spanish restaurant in Newark, he replied.

"Newark?" Cherry said. "Why not Mongolia?"

Newark. He wasn't going into New York City. Not yet.

Remembering Alvarado leaping from the trunk, he took the train out of Philadelphia, arrived two hours early and went inside the restaurant, rummaging around like a health inspector.

Goldsworthy was there too. He called to report Bleak's movements. Said he was wearing a blue blazer, white oxford, black jeans, trainers. He was yellowed here and there from a beating, and he had a nasty cut across his lip. No, he couldn't detect a weapon.

"Mr. Bleak," Cherry said when he sat.

Goldsworthy was in a banquette across the room. He carried a Sig Sauer P238 and the compact pistol sat snug in the palm of his right hand resting on his thigh.

"You sure did make a mess of things," Cherry said as he unfurled his napkin.

"Fernando Alvarado tried to kill her."

"He overreacted."

"And Kwame Green?"

An '87 Vega Sicilia Unico Reserva arrived.

Cherry wanted a cheeseburger, but settled on a skirt steak, moo rare.

"Kwame Green," Cherry said. "Taylor McHugh is sending his family forty-eight thousand dollars. Maybe more, I don't know. It's bullshit, but what can you do?"

"You're hoping Carlos Alvarado didn't tell anyone about you—"

"Speaking of which, did he give you all that?" Cherry ran a circle near his own face. "I can see why you killed him."

"That's your play if I make a call about Green?"

"The West Allis cops know to look at Alvarado," Cherry said. "Maybe their friends in LAPD find the gun in his house."

Maybe they find a gun on his sister too.

"Taylor set you up?" Cherry asked.

"Taylor's good at that," he replied, his fingers on the butter knife.

"What do you think? She does a decade working Legal Aid? Or better yet, you send her a card every Christmas. Love, John Bleak."

Cherry held up the wine bottle.

He declined.

Cherry poured like he wanted a head on it.

"So…"

The envelopes sat in his inside pocket. All along he knew he wasn't going to let McHugh get away with it. Cole said it: McHugh had mentored her. She told her it was important to seize opportunity. McHugh's opportunity started when she set up her former secretary for a beating.

He didn't want Cherry to get away with it either and time didn't matter.

"What else?" Cherry asked.

"Mary Louise Szarsynski."

"Who?"

"No," he said. "Let's close this thing."

"I'm telling you I don't know who she is. Why should I care?"

"Just like that…"

Cherry raised his glass. "All honor and glory to her for coming up with you."

"And her family?"

"Sure. Why not?"

He studied Cherry.

"Best I can do, Bleak," Cherry said. "You're not getting it in writing."

He put the envelopes on the table.

He stood.

He left.

Cherry hefted the envelopes. He looked across the room at Goldsworthy and shook his head.

Goldsworthy sat back and lifted his cell.

"Let him go," he told the two guys he had out on Market Street.

Then he came over and carefully lifted the butter knife stained with John Bleak's fingerprints. Cherry nodded as Goldsworthy slipped it into a plastic bag.

"Rainy day," Cherry said, his cheek plump with his garlic steak, blood sluicing along his fingers.

Goldsworthy moved the bag toward a jacket pocket.

"No," Cherry said without looking up. He held out his hand. "Give."

Goldsworthy surrendered the bag.

"Now go to your room," Cherry said. "Think about what you've done."

Stung, Goldsworthy hung his head. He walked off in a cloud of bitterness and shame.

He used a pay phone in Newark's Penn Station.

He said, "It's all right."

"Sam, are you sure?"

"Yes."

He hung up and walked toward the ticket booth.

They asked for ID.

J.J. Walk, Toronto, South Dakota.

The guy said, "I didn't know there was a Toronto in South Dakota…"

Cole K. Bennett heard a knock on her door.

Her heart jumped.

Rising slowly from the bed, she hit the mute button on the TV clicker.

Her carryall, packed and ready, rested on the lone chair in the room.

For the past week, every move she made was governed by his advice. When she went out for meals, she heard his voice. Passing a stranger a second time on the street, his voice. At the hotel health club, his voice. She drove to the Larimer Lounge to catch a band, blending into the crowd. His voice.

Holding her breath, she went on her toes to look through the peephole.

She yanked open the door.

"Mom!" she shouted.

Rosy with love and forgiveness, Judy Szarsynski held out her arms. "Sweetie, Sam told me it's all right."

It's all right, Mary Louise thought as they hugged good and tight. Oh yeah, it's way better than all right.

The driver wanted the West Side, to circle the Battery, but Cherry couldn't wait. Canal, he told him, to Broadway.

Canal's a nightmare, boss.

Cherry put him out on West Street and jumped behind the wheel.

Canal Street was a nightmare.

Cherry kept looking at the two envelopes on the passenger's seat. It took a deep dip in his reservoir of discipline to avoid ripping them open as he waited.

Up ahead, traffic was blocked by street-crossing waves of Chinese men and women, each 105 years old, teetering, plastic bags plump with vegetables in their crinkled fists.

Maybe I'm a genius, Cherry was thinking, but me, I put a pedestrian bridge over this place. Maybe an escalator, a tollgate at the entrance, 20 yuans to cross. Thirty-five round-trip.

Eventually, he made it to Broadway. Cops were checking trucks that were headed below Liberty Street. Traffic stacked again.

Oh fuck this.

Cherry put the car in a bus stop in front of the last department store in lower Manhattan. He called the driver.

"You want your job back?"

Ten minutes later, he stormed into his suite, his shirt so sweat-soaked it dripped.

Secretaries scurried for cover.

The CFO of Norwegian Gas & Hydropower ASA and two deputies were waiting in his private conference room. Coffee had been served on china.

"Out," said Cherry.

Shocked, they reminded him they had flown from Oslo for the meeting. They were eager for his counsel: because he was enterprising, subtle in his aggression and a meritocratic egalitarian — who met with as many subordinates as Francis Cherry? — they assumed a shared heritage.

"But Mr. Cherry—"

"Go to Macy's," he said. "See a show."

He banged the door shut.

He mopped his brow with his tie.

He sat.

The big envelope had held his skip money. He thought maybe he'd had $80,000 in thousand-dollar bills in it, enough to get him to his stash in the Caymans. Could've been a few more, a few less. He didn't know. The bills were unmarked and nonsequential, meaning Szarsynski would've had no trouble off-loading them. Kwame Green's family shouldn't either.

Yielding his letter opener, he sliced the flap on one of the small envelopes.

Out tumbled his passport and an American Express black card.

If he had to go, he could go.

He didn't give a shit that Szarsynski swiped them — they were easily replaced — other than she made him look vulnerable. He didn't want the Street to know he could be taken. Hence, he gave the job to Goldsworthy and not some downtown security firm packed with ex-CIA and Mossad operatives.

There's a lesson in there somewhere, he told himself.

His hands shook.

Finally, the second envelope was open.

He let its contents flutter to the desktop.

A black-and-white photo taken in the late '50s.

A lock of baby hair, tied with a violet bow.

Cherry sighed as he lifted the photo and tilted it toward the light.

The woman was plump with a child and sad-eyed despite her smile, the man short and seemingly stern. They posed before the steps of a tenement on a summer day. The man wore his lone suit, the woman a floral dress and sensible shoes. His parents held their hats in their hands.

He stroked the lock of his hair with his thumb and forefinger.

Wilshire Boulevard was Sunday afternoon quiet. Everything closed, no traffic, at least none to speak of. White marble awash in sunlight, a few people strolling toward the Laemmle Music Hall for a picture from Iran, another from Singapore. Soaring palm trees sagged. Michael Koons sat under an umbrella at a table for two outside a café, an onion bagel on wax paper, scallion cream cheese, tea; a tiny man who couldn't gain weight if he tried. He sat his cell phone on the tabletop, glanced at the time. His black Audi coupe sparkled at the curb.

Koons, who wore a canary-yellow shirt and pale gray slacks, looked this way, that way, sipped his tea. He removed his sunglasses, pinched the bridge of his nose. He looked at the clock in his phone. He heard.

Pup came spiraling onto Wilshire, tilting just so for momentum, now knees bent, her skateboard rattling on the concrete. She rode past the antique shop and the nail salon, gliding with ease. When she reached Koons' table, she stopped and the board leaped into her arms.

"Isabel," said Koons as he stood.

Pup had her hood up and drawn to her face. Koons struggled to kiss her cheek. As it was he had to go on his toes. She was brushing up against 6 feet. Model tall, thin but not sickly so, a beauty. With a stud in her nose, another high on her ear, her hair under the hood granny-apple green.

Koons pulled out the seat for her, but she sat at the table next to his. They faced sunny Wilshire.

"The hair," he said, "it's new, isn't it?"

Isabel Jellico kept one of her purple Chuck Taylors on the skateboard, rolling it back, forth. She wore khaki cargo pants. She undid the zipper on the black hoodie to reveal a pale gray T-shirt with a faded drawing of Felix the Cat.

"What's up, Michael?" The studs were magnets. There was no chance that she would pierce her body to ride a trend. Bad enough she'd dyed her hair for the charade. "News?"

In fact, Koons had news, but he wasn't sharing it yet. Some of the funding for her Nathaniel Hill project might dry up. Canal+ was having second thoughts. They heard the female lead, born in Haute-Normandie, was unhappy. Koons knew she had a shot at a bigger role in a project at DreamWorks, one with global potential.

"It's about your father," he said.

Pup stood.

"Wait. It's not him. Not exactly."

She stared at Koons. "Don't tell me. How many times—"

"No. No."

"Apocalyptic, Michael."

He waved his little hands. "No, no, no, no. No. Listen."

For the past hour, she'd cased the neighborhood, circling in her eight-year-old Nissan, then setting up in a pharmacy across the street, to make sure her father hadn't tailed her, wasn't coming. This after spending the past week looking out from behind the counter at the coffee shop, darting to class and sleeping on a sofa in a lounge in Dogwood Hall. "'Not exactly.' What does that mean?"

"I want you to know what I know."

"Michael..."

"It's not repeating what he said or claimed. It's just that... You know Mary-Karl, don't you?"

Pup nodded. An agent in Michael's office. Mary-Karl. She couldn't picture her, though. There were so many people. All these people: What do they want?

"Come on, Isabel. Sit. Have something to drink."

She went into the café. She came out with an orange Fanta and a plastic cup of ice, sliding change into a pouch.

"Mary-Karl said she was driving through Eagle Rock and she saw your father."

Pup poured the soda pop into the cup. Koons heard it hiss.

"He was carrying bags of ice to a car. Mary-Karl said he was beaten pretty badly. Limping. Bleeding." Koons made a gesture near his head. "All swollen. Bruises."

Pup turned away.

"I'm just reporting what she saw, Isabel. I didn't want it getting back to you."

"How does she even know him?"

"I told you. He came to the restaurant."

She sipped her drink.

Koons said, "Remember, he said you were in danger and then what Mary-Karl saw. Two and two, right? Maybe he was protecting you?"

She said, "What do you want from me, Michael?"

"Whatever happened, he didn't try to put that on us. When he called to say it was all clear, he was gone."

Pup turned to face him.

He said, "I know. I know. It's not my business. I hear you; I heard you. But I want you happy, sweetie. I don't know what to do."

"You don't have to do anything, Michael," she said.

He saw she had orange lips from the beverage.

"But — and please, I'm not interfering; whatever you want is whatever you want. But he cares, Isabel."

"I don't."

"Oh sweetie. Please. You have—"

"Michael. This is non-negotiable. If you need to feel good about it, all right. You made your pitch."

"I'm not trying to upset you."

"I'm not upset. But I'm not going to say this again. He has no place in my life. He made his choices, I've made mine."

Koons sighed. "OK, Isabel."

"OK. Good then."

They sat in silence, Koons lifting, then setting aside his tepid tea.

"Let me see your face," he said, forcing a smile.

Pup dropped her hood.

"You look sad, sweetie."

"I'm not sad," she said as the hood went up again.

Soon she was paddling along Wilshire, going away, one sneaker on the concrete to propel her. Soon she waggled with both feet on board, leaned to turn and disappeared down a side street.

He left the Amtrak station in St. Paul. He walked five miles along the river to the city center in Minneapolis. He bought six shirts. He was cold, so he picked out a sweater to wear under his blazer.

As he passed the dressing room, he saw the scar on his lip. He knew it wasn't going to look any better than it did now.

The light rail line took him from downtown, past the airport and all the way to the Mall of America.

He rode for hours.

People came and went.

He tried to put the blinders back on. To step back into the fog.

It was impossible to try to forget.

He told himself to let everything go.

He could do it.

He could do it.

Under the padding of his left sneaker was the driver's license and Social Security card the marshals had given him; under the padding on the right, his real license and passport.

Late morning turned to afternoon.

It was a beautiful day, the sun star-bursting on the glass-and-steel towers downtown.

People were happy. They liked it here. It was their hometown.

He ran his tongue along the porcelain bridge in the side of his mouth.

He had grilled rainbow trout under a sugar-maple tree in Minnehaha Park. He finished a novel while he ate. He started another.

The waitress told him she got off at seven.

He listened to the waterfall.

Back on the light rail, he fell asleep. He dreamed. Clouds rushed through the sky. He had to be there, but where?

He saw a courthouse, sweeping stairs, columns. Moira was walking down the steps in front of him. They'd done what they had to do. Pup held his hand. Everything was going to be all right.

Her blood sprayed, staining construction paper pinned to a corkboard. Her handprint in blood on the desk. Her eyes open, staring at the ceiling. Her throat cut from ear to ear. The killer's boot heel crushed the video.

He jumped, waking to find he was back downtown in Minneapolis.

Evening had settled in.

He dug his phone out of his jeans.

Nobody called.

#

ABOUT THE AUTHOR

Photo by Andrei Jackamets

Jim Fusilli is a native of Hoboken, New Jersey, which serves as a model for the city of Narrows Gate in his fiction. A graduate of St. Peter's College, he joined *The Wall Street Journal* in the early 1980s and has been the newspaper's rock and pop music critic since 2008. He is the author of six novels and numerous short stories. He and his wife, public-relations executive Diane Holuk Fusilli, live in New York City. They have one daughter.